ABOUT THE AUTHOR

Kayleigh Evans is from a valley in South Wales – the perfect backdrop for the *Serendipity Valley* series. After writing for many years, Kayleigh decided to share her works with other likeminded authors before taking the plunge in to the world of publishing. *Serendipity Valley: How It Begins* is her debut novel in the series. For more information, visit:

KayleighEvansAuthor.com

SERENDIPITY VALLEY

VALLEY

How It Begins

KAYLEIGH EVANS

Serendipity Valley
How It Begins

First Edition 2023

Ebook ISBN: 978-1-7384243-0-6
Audiobook ISBN: 978-1-7384243-4-4
Paperback ISBN: 978-1-7384243-1-3
Hardback ISBN: 978-1-7384243-2-0
Large Print ISBN: 978-1-7384243-3-7

Category: Women's Fiction

ACKNOWLEDGMENTS

Writing this book is one of my most significant achievements. Without trying to be excessive, I honestly need to thank every person who has been on this amazing journey with me. My family and friends have helped fuel my imagination and I am extremely fortunate. In particular, I am forever indebted to those who fact-checked me (you know who you are).

The publishing of this book all started with setting up the YHLP writing group in the most enjoyable coffee shop in which you could hope to sit and write. Teleri Jones at Yr Hen Lyfrgell – The Old Library – you are the best!

I'm grateful to be surrounded by such creative and helpful authors and especially appreciative to Alison Morris and Victoria Mullins for their invaluable insights. You are wonderful.

I also want to give a very special thank you to Daniel Parsons for being a brilliant editor and for sharing your profound knowledge to support your fellow writers.

And lastly, for you lovely readers; thank you for purchasing my book. I hope you love the characters as much as I do. I can't wait to share the rest of their journey with you.

THE LIFE OF A VALLEY RIVER

Starting from a spring, a curious river roams.
It flows down the middle of the glacial valley,
A place we call our home.

On the mountains we have farmland,
Livestock that eats the grass that grows.
Towns and villages pressed to the hillsides,
Rows descending to the river's flow.

The river meets its little brother.
They run past a country park.
Till they come across a greater river,
all together they embark.

No longer in a valley,
They follow a manmade trail.
A friend joins them en route to the city before,
They empty into the bay.

Waters that took every chance,
A life that did not waste.
The water may travel back somehow,
But forever, it is changed.

PROLOGUE

"Whose great idea was it to come to the park on our lunch break?" Brooke huffed as she destroyed the lush green grass beneath her feet.

In an attempt to get mud off her shoes, she vigorously rubbed them against the thick blades to little avail.

Jenny laughed. The muddy patch Brooke managed to stand in should have completely dried; the air was warm and the sun was shining. It was just Brooke's luck that the mud was wet, and it now caked her shoes.

"Blame the love birds," Cam replied. That was how he referred to Matthew and Kelly. Picking up the nearest stick, he threw it into the tall, thick bushes that lined the path. "They can't go kissing in school now, can they?"

"Just because you're jealous, Cam" Matthew retaliated. Walking with his arm draped over Kelly's shoulders, Matthew turned his attention to Ethan who walked beside them. "He can't get a girlfriend see, Eth. He's jealous you have all the girls after you."

Ethan chuckled at the retort.

"Cam's got lots of girlfriends, actually," Jenny chimed in.

"Including you?" Matthew raised an eyebrow.

"Don't be so silly," Cam dismissed the claim, walking backwards to face them. "Jenny's way out of my league, and besides, Dan fancies her."

There was a chorus of "oohs."

Jenny felt Ethan's eyes on her and shot Cam a glare, warning him not to say another word.

"Oh, be quiet all of you," Brooke demanded. "It's all about who fancies who with you lot. Does no one care if my shoes are

3

ruined? My mother's going to go mad!"

They all snickered.

"You're better off waiting for the mud to dry, Brooke. It'll fall off." Ethan suggested. "Won't take long in this weather."

Jenny knew Ethan worked on his parents' farm and probably had lots of experience with muddy shoes.

"Or… I can wash them in the stream for you if you like?" Cam offered Brooke, grinning.

"As if I'd trust you with my shoes – not on your life!"

"Suit yourself." Cam shrugged. Then, leaning towards her, he tapped her on the arm. "Tag, you're it."

Forgetting about her muddy shoes, Brooke sped after him along the path that led to the opening of Hardd Park. Like a whippet, Cam had gone and had left her for dust, speeding towards the playground. So, Brooke turned her attention to the others – slow and easy targets – tagging Kelly.

"This is sooo childish!" Kelly groaned before chasing after Matthew, who in turn tagged Ethan.

Jenny laughed. Kelly was the youngest one – fifteen. The rest of them were now sixteen but they still couldn't resist a game of tag. There wasn't much else to do in the Valley at their age. Jenny was the last one left. Trying to remain untagged, she ran off-path around the trees to dodge Ethan.

Out of obstacles to run around, Ethan started to gain on her. He took a confident dive to touch her back, all while her school shoes slid on the damp ground. She heard a thump but didn't feel Ethan's hand touch her back.

Laughing and out of breath, she slowed and turned to see his face planted on the floor.

"Missed me," she teased, brushing away the hair that clung to her face.

"Did not, totally tagged you!" he argued, grinning as he stood.

Noticing the others were already in the playground, Jenny didn't want the game to end.

"Race to the swings as a tie break?" she offered.

"Deal. From this tree? He moved beside her and put himself in a runner's stance. She rolled her eyes as he started announcing: "Ready… steady…"

4

Jenny sprinted as fast as she could before he said "go" but it was only a couple of seconds before his long legs started to overtake her. Watching him follow the footworn path, Jenny slowed as the surface beneath her feet became uneven. She was surely beaten now.

As Ethan neared the gate, however, his perfect running form faltered. His foot hit a rock and his momentum sent his legs hurtling over his head. Jenny heard him laughing as he turned on to his back, recovering from the flip. Hoping to take advantage of his misfortune, she re-accelerated and sprinted past him towards the gate.

Getting up just in time, though, Ethan grabbed her foot, causing her to sprawl on the floor ahead of him. Jenny strained trying to look up, the park gate was only an arm's length away. Her school uniform would get ruined but she crawled, panting and laughing as Ethan held on to her leg. His grip moved as he struggled to get up. So, seeing an opportunity, she kicked her leg free and scrambled to her feet.

"Go, Jenny!" Cam shouted, clearly entertained.

"No – go, Ethan!" Matthew cheered.

"Woohoo!" Kelly joined in.

The usually quiet park was full of whoops and hollers as they both tried to squeeze through the narrow, yellow kissing gate. Overtaking him by inches, Jenny touched her fingertips to the swing bars.

"He let you win," scoffed Matthew from the bench, his arm still draped over Kelly.

Both red-faced and panting, Jenny looked up at Ethan and their eyes met. He turned to the others and shook his head.

"Fair and square" he announced, holding up his hands. Walking towards the empty swing next to her, he paused before sitting down. "I'm not seeing who can swing the highest, before you ask."

Jenny laughed. "Did you enjoy your trip?"

"The best one I've ever been on." His eyes glinted in the sun as he kicked off to swing.

"The mud fell off my shoe!" Brooke cried out in excitement from the middle of the climbing ropes. Her body bobbed as she tried to balance and inspect her shoes.

At the same time, a phone ringtone sounded.

"Oh, Jen, your phone is still in my pocket." Brooke fumbled to retrieve it, the ringing sound echoing through the now quieting park. Holding the phone in the air as if Jenny could see the screen, she called, "Dan is trying to ring you!"

Aware of Ethan watching her, Jenny avoided his gaze, hoping she still looked red from running rather than embarrassment. She sighed before shouting back to Brooke, "Just text him, 'I'll talk to him later' or something."

Ethan abandoned the swing and, without so much as a glance at her, signalled Matthew.

"Longest holding on to the monkey bars wins?"

Pulling away from his embrace with Kelly, Matthew stood. "Heck yeah!"

Jenny slowed her swing to an almost stop, causing an anticlimactic squeaking noise, fitting for how she felt.

CHAPTER 1

It was almost 3:15 pm. Jenny couldn't wait to wrap up the school day and have her pupils race through the goodbye song so she could finish work. Turning eighteen was a promise of fun and independence. No one ever mentioned, though, that it would also mean working with people you may not like to earn money for said fun and independence.

Looking around the colourful classroom, she inspected the handmade displays that brightened the room and let out a sigh. Joanne, the other nursery nurse, had been working with the class teacher Mrs Green for over five years. Jenny had been working with her for less than five months and already, she couldn't wait never to see her again.

Pulling her attention back to writing the number four as an open four on her observation sheet, she recalled the first scolding: *We can't confuse the children by writing numbers incorrectly. It's unprofessional.*

Jenny wanted to attest that the children would never see the closed number fours in her handwritten notes but she'd bit her tongue. Still, the scolding's didn't stop. Only the camaraderie between her and Joanne helped her withstand the sour outbursts and criticisms.

> *Is there a reason the paintings aren't dry?*
> *Jagged edges are completely unsuitable.*
> *Our pupils need competent staff!*

Spotting Brody pausing mid-song to pick his nose, Jenny tore her thoughts away from the not-so-pleasant memories and grinned. One sharp look from Mrs Green was all it took for Brody to sit upright. He began singing once more, even louder than he had before, as if making up for his pause. Jenny stifled a chuckle.

Mrs Green reminded Jenny of a Victorian children's governess she had once seen in a film: cold and strict. The battleaxe gave her the same look she just gave Brody. She was doing it now, prompting Jenny to resume writing up the last of her notes.

"At half-past three we go home for tea, or maybe at quarter to four..." chorused through the classroom.

Jenny sang along with mixed emotions. Rising to return the observation book to the locked cupboards, she caught sight of Joanne returning from the stockroom with the same look of relief she felt about it being the end of the day.

Dismissed, the children rushed for their cardigans and bags. Jenny and Joanne made their way to the corridor to help them.

"I'm going to have fish fingers and chips tonight, Miss," Rosy beamed up at Jenny.

"That sounds delicious. Can I come for tea, too?" Rosy laughed at the idea. Popping closed the top button on the little girl's cardigan, Jenny grinned. "Have a lovely weekend, Rosy."

Rosy waved and ran off to her waiting Mother.

"You too, Miss! see you Monday," she called back. Knowing she would not see Rosy or any of the other children again made Jenny's heart ache.

Returning to the now-silent classroom, she heard Joanne fumbling in the cloakroom. A moment later, she appeared, holding a wine bag and gifts from the other staff.

"Please don't leave me," she pleaded and handed over the assortment.

Overcome with emotion, Jenny placed the gifts down on one of the small tables and hugged her friend.

"I'm sorry, I'll miss you," she managed before Mrs Green entered the classroom. There was an awkward pause.

"Ah yes. Goodbye, Jenny." Mrs Green's jet-black bob whipped around as fast as she did, back out of the room.

Joanne rolled her eyes and Jenny giggled.

"Thanks for all this. You didn't have to."

Joanne fanned her face. "I won't cry, I won't cry!" Totally, crying, she wiped water from the corner of her eyes. "Right, come on, you. Get yourself home or you'll be late for the night out! No time to wallow. You have a new job Monday. Get that fun out of your system."

Jenny laughed, scooping up her gifts. She wished she could take Joanne with her but she couldn't. All she could do was press the buzzer and let herself out of the school for the last time.

A wave of nostalgia washed over Jenny as she got off the bus. Looking at Primrose Drive, she drank in the details of the place where she grew up. It hadn't changed one bit and she hoped it never would. Jenny still lived with her Mam and Dad at the bottom of the hill and Cam still lived opposite with his Mam and Kelly.

Water fights, street parties, being told off for riding skateboards down the steep hill. Memories whirled through her mind as she walked the curve in the road, descending into the street.

Doreen, her elderly neighbour who lived on the brow of the hill was standing on a ladder. It rested on the porch of the house and Jenny watched Doreen wipe her brow in the heat, using her free hand to clutch onto the rickety ladder.

Shaking her head, Jenny followed the pavement until Doreen spotted her. The old woman waved, the ladder shuddering beneath her.

"It's a warm one today, isn't it, love?"

"Definitely is," Jenny called back.

"Good for my tomatoes, though."

"Let me know if you need any help picking them again this year, or weeding your hanging baskets."

Jenny offered, she couldn't help but worry about Doreen – always up a ladder or carting about tools at her age.

"Oh, you're a good girl," Doreen responded. "I'll give you and Cameron 'a shout' as they say."

Jenny laughed. "You be careful. We don't want you to fall."

Doreen waved her hand dismissively. "We're still nimble enough, don't you worry. Our gardening keeps us young."

9

Giving Jenny a nod, Doreen turned her attention back to the colourful hanging basket and resumed her weed hunt.

Jenny's mother always said Doreen and Bert had it best with their house on the brow of the hill. They had light all year round and they didn't have to struggle in the snow. The couple weren't able to have children. So, the garden was their baby, and the love and affection they gave it showed. Even in the winter, flowers bloomed across the lawn despite the cold, gloomy weather.

Jenny liked being at the bottom of the street. The house was barricaded with large beech trees where bramble bushes had formed a wall in front of thick tree trunks. A little lane ran beside her house leading to a small hidden mountain stream. Her and Cam used to race grass boats down it and catch tadpoles in the pools. The only thing she disliked was the lack of view. From the top of the street you had a panoramic one. West was the head of the valley and from there your eyes could follow the landscape and the river leading all the way down towards the city.

She would often walk to the top of the street to contemplate and let her mind wander. Her thoughts went back to when she and Cam would sit up there to watch the streetlamps across the valley flick on and twinkle like magic. The warm smell of tarmac dragged her thoughts away from the cooler nights to the boiling hot day.

She tuned in to the sound of loud male voices emanating from Cam's back garden. His gate was closed but she guessed everyone was over early. Excited to get ready to join them, she rushed up the driveway, determined that tonight she was going to let her hair down.

CHAPTER 2

Ethan only ever got to see the guys when he wasn't busy working on the farm. With them all busy finishing college, getting together was a rare occasion. He hadn't seen Jenny Griffiths in over a year. Seeing her enter the house opposite Cam's left him feeling bewildered. Jenny was always spending time with her boyfriend but he had heard she had broken up with Dan a while ago. Did *she have a new boyfriend? Does he live opposite Cam?*

Her smile had always piqued his curiosity and her sense of humour made him want to get to know her better. He never did, though. The same friends were all they shared. Jenny always had someone interested in her and he hadn't been out with the group for a while.

After a gruelling day on the farm, he was grateful to be having drinks to unwind. Stepping out through the patio doors, into the heat, he joined the group formed around the garden table.

Kelly was sitting on Matthew's lap and Cam was laughing at Brooke, who was failing terribly at trying to flip a cup.

"Another beer, Eth?" Kelly rose from Matthew's lap and walked towards the ice bucket that sat next to the BBQ.

"That would be great, thanks."

He took it from her and gulped, hoping it would cool him down. His skin was used to the sun on the farm but there was no breeze in Cam's garden.

"I've given Jenny a text, Cam. She should be joining us for pre-drinks soon." Kelly stated.

Ethan's ears pricked up at the sound of her name. Taking another drink, he demonstrated the technique for how to flip

11

the cup to Brooke.

"Haven't seen Jenny in ages. What's she up to these days, Cam?" he asked as casually as he could.

"Not much. Just this and that," a sweet voice answered in place of Cam's.

Jenny stood at the garden gate behind him, still wearing some sort of uniform but her hair was now flowing around her shoulders. Her smile was as pleasing as her voice.

"How are you doing, Eth?"

She was a lot more confident than he remembered.

"Yeah, good, thanks."

She nodded as he cleared his throat. Then she looked a Cam. "Mam's asking if you've sorted a taxi to get us home. She can pick us up otherwise."

Ethan couldn't help but watch as she lingered by the gate. He suspected he looked as different to her as she did to him.

"Good old Tracey," Cam laughed taking another drink. "She and Mam will be pleased. There's a taxi rank there. They can have their wine."

"Perfect." Tapping the gate with her fingers, Jenny gave them an awkward wave and disappeared.

"Jenny lives across the road." Kelly enlightened Ethan.

Ethan nodded, relieved. So, Jenny didn't have a boyfriend living opposite. *Maybe she was single? How did he not know she lived opposite Cam and Kelly?*

"Our Mothers share a bottle of wine together every Friday night, she's practically a sibling to us," Cam added, looking over to Kelly. "The ramblings we've had to put up with, isn't that right, Kel?"

Uninterested, Kelly said nothing.

Ignoring her cold shoulder, Cam headed for a ping pong table stationed in the garden.

"Game of beer pong, anyone?"

***

As Jenny left the house, actually joining the party this time, the sound of music from Cam's Garden drifted through the air. The closer she got, the clearer the song became. Someone was singing "The Mack" and she hummed along as she approached the gate.

12

Cam and Ethan were playing beer pong against Kelly and Matthew, while Brooke watched on in amusement.

Seeing Ethan earlier stirred up feelings Jenny couldn't comprehend. Since the day she beat him to the swings, Ethan always left her with the impression he wanted to avoid her. She felt the opposite about him, though. The way he had looked at her while she stood by the gate earlier made her stomach twist in anticipation.

Her mind was full of him as she returned to the house. Many of the girls desired him in school, including her.

Watching him concentrate on the tense beer pong game that was underway, she realised how much he had changed. He was almost as tall as Cam who had always been taller than average. Taking in the way his dark blonde hair flopped over his forehead, she admired his eyes fixing on their target. His face was steady and serious.

The ball plopped in one of the cups on the opposite end of the table, splashing beer at Kelly who shrieked.

Jenny watched Cam and Ethan bounce around, hugging each other in celebration over their victory.

Kelly and Matthew grimaced then laughed at the four cups left to drink. Jenny walked over to the table to take a seat next to Brooke who was absorbed in her phone.

Cam walked over and put his hand on her shoulder.

"Drink, Madam?"

"Why, thank you, Sir," she responded with a smirk. "On the rocks?"

Cam's brow was sweaty in the heat. He wiped himself with the towel hanging off the back of his chair before heading to the kitchen inside,

"Anyone else want a top-up?" he called before going through the patio doors.

"I'll grab one, thanks," called Ethan.

"Me too!" said Brooke. Head no longer buried in her phone, she spotted Jenny. "Oh, hi Jen. Sorry." She leaned in to give her a brief hug. "I'll come help you with the drinks, Cam."

Kelly and Matthew were still making their way through the cups so Ethan joined Jenny at the table.

"Hi." He flashed her a charming smile and sat down opposite her. "Long time no see."

Trying to read his face she nodded.

"Yeah, I haven't seen you in ages. Still working on the farm?"

Ethan looked over the varnished garden fence to a view of Bryn Farm on the opposite hillside. "Yeah, I think Dad's gearing me up to take the reins."

Jenny was unable to gauge if this was something he wanted. Finding it difficult to read his expression, she followed his gaze taking in the view.

Rows of houses zig-zagged upwards from the bottom of the valley. They stopped just before the large open fields that encompassed the rest of the hillside. Jenny could just about see the shapes of the horses, Welsh Black cattle and white dots of sheep grazing in their fields.

"That sounds great. Is it something you want to do?"

Ethan shrugged. "It wouldn't be the worst thing in the world." Turning his head to look at her, he asked, "So, what's this and that you're up to then?"

Jenny drew her eyes away from him and back to the view, her cheeks filling with heat. He was giving her his full attention.

"Just working. I have a new job in an intervention company, starting Monday."

Ethan nodded with a confused expression on his face. "Congratulations."

Their eyes met and the butterflies in Jenny's stomach turned to fizz. They both looked away as quickly as they had looked up. Glancing back at him, she saw he was smiling.

"A game, Jen?" The question came from Cam as he returned with drinks in his hand. "Me and Brooke versus you and Ethan?"

He gave her a wink and walked over to the ping pong table, not giving her chance to respond. Looking over to Ethan who was rising from his chair, Jenny shot him an anxious glance.

"Don't worry, Jen. I'm sure we'll win. We're on the same team this time." He said playfully.

"You might hold me back," she teased, joining them at the table where Cam was setting up fresh drinking cups.

They lost the game of beer pong.

Jenny and Ethan stood as Kelly and Matthew did before them, drinking four of the six cups of cider and beer. Admitting

14

defeat, they winced and laughed at what they were expected to drink.

"Taxi's here," Kelly called from the garden gate.

Feeling tipsy, Ethan and Jenny shared a mischievous look.

"Think we should do it?" she asked him.

"Let's just take them in the taxi." Ethan grabbed the remaining cups.

"Very sensible." Jenny giggled and followed him to the waiting minibus.

CHAPTER 3

The club was noisy and averting Ethan's gaze was proving difficult. Biting down on her straw, Jenny tried to concentrate on the group conversation, often failing, her mind overtaken with interest.

Allowing herself to glance up at him sitting opposite her in the booth, she found him looking at her with amusement. The skin on her arms prickled and she remembered the feel of his skin brushing against hers in the minibus. Her body was flooded with a reaction she had never felt before. She had no idea how the night was going to end but she hoped she would find out.

"Any more drinks?" Cam offered, getting up to go to the bar.

"Boring!" Brooke declared arriving at the best possible moment with a tray of shots in hand.

"You're all still talking? Why are we not dancing yet?" She put down the tray, handing a shot to Cam who shrugged,

"I guess it's shot-and-dance time". Jenny eyed her suspiciously. Brooke gave her a sheepish look back and joined the others, taking a shot from the tray.

"To many nights out like this," Matthew toasted. They lifted the shot glasses, sharing a laugh at the fatuous statement before knocking back the black liquid. The lights near the booth were dim but seemed bright compared to the dark of the dancefloor. Only neon lights whirling around the room allowed them to see the silhouettes of the dancers already there.

"Right. Come on, everyone – up!" Brooke started pulling at their arms until everyone was moving out of the booth, heading towards the dancefloor.

One song faded into the next. Jenny threw her hands up with everyone else on the dancefloor. Catching sight of Ethan coming through the crowd, her stomach twisted. *God, he was gorgeous.*

Turning to distract herself, she found Brooke dancing provocatively with a group of boys next to them. As she rolled her eyes and laughed, hands snaked around her waist. Her head spun, thinking of Ethan's hands wrapping around her. Still moving to the music, she turned to see Cam with his prankster grin and his eyes full of laughter. Grabbing his arms, she moved them away and danced backwards, a stern look on her face.

"Bet you're disappointed, eh?" He winked before taking her hand and placing it in Ethan's who had just about made it through the crowded dancefloor.

Ethan gave her a twirl. When she stopped spinning, they felt still compared to the movement around them. No one seemed to take notice of what felt like fireworks and dizzying bangs going off between them.

He looked down at her. Was he thinking of going in for a kiss? A jolt of electricity surged through her body. He grabbed at her hips and pulled her closer to him. Mixed with lust and alcohol, she was grateful he had a steady grip, otherwise, she might have fallen.

***

"You okay, Jen?" Ethan moved backwards, observing her. He kept hold of her hips, like he was the only thing keeping her steady. She looked pale and her bright eyes had a wild look to them.

Jenny pulled away from him and turned, moving quickly towards the stairs at the back of the club. Not sure what was happening, Ethan looked at Brooke who was too busy dancing.

"I'm going to go check on Jenny!" he called to Cam over the loud music. Cam nodded and raised his bottle in response.

The crowds leaving the toilets and coming down the stairs were slowing Jenny's progress. Ethan's eyes were fixed on her and he took the stairs two at a time. Reaching the corridor at the top of the stairs, he was worried he wouldn't reach her in time and called out, "Jen, wait!"

Jenny stopped and turned around.

"Jen, are you okay?' People passed by her on either side, bumping into his shoulder. Jenny stood still, her eyes sparkling, watching him.

Now standing close to her, he went to speak. Before he could, though, she put a finger on his lips. Everything slowed as she rose to meet him on her tiptoes, replacing her finger with her lips, and the most delicate of kisses.

Not being able to help himself, he pressed harder into her mouth, he was unable to hear the passers-by making "ooo" noises and catcalls as their lips locked again and again. He didn't care; she took up all his senses... until Jenny stepped back.

"I won't be long," she whispered breathlessly and headed towards the women's toilets.

As he watched her go, the sounds of hollers and wolf whistles slowly crept into his thoughts. Moving out of the steady flow of people heading to and from the toilets, he was utterly dumbfounded. When they brushed arms earlier, his attraction to her amplified but he didn't expect anything to happen tonight. Jenny had given him the signal he needed to pursue her now, but was she acting differently to earlier?

The minutes he waited in the corridor, perched on the windowsill, turned to nearly half an hour. Wondering if he had missed her coming out of the ladies' room, he wandered back down the stairs. Most of the group were still on the dancefloor. Kelly was sitting in their booth so he joined her.

"Seen Jenny?" he sat down, facing her,

"No. Only when you followed her up to the loos. What did you two get up to? You've been a while?" Kelly waggled her eyebrows playfully.

"She went in but I didn't see her come out. Just wanted to check she was okay. Sure you haven't seen her?" he asked again to be certain.

"No, I'm sure. She's just probably found someone to dance with. Those boys Brooke was dancing with bought them drinks earlier." Kelly took off her bright pink heel and rubbed her foot. "My poor feet are broken in these heels."

She threw the heels on the seat next to her and began to rummage through her bag. Ethan took his cue and left for the bar. Smiling at the pretty barmaid who blushed as she served him, he mulled over the questions in his head. *Where could Jenny be? She wouldn't avoid me and find someone else to dance with, surely?*

Scanning the dance floor one more time, he frowned. Could he have read things wrong? He winked at the barmaid and thanked her before wandering back to the group. Cam would know where Jenny was. Jenny always went to Cam.

***

Putting the empty glass bottles in the bin, Gemma couldn't believe her luck. The handsome guy she served earlier invited her out after work. Grabbing her bag, she felt a rush of excitement and said farewell to her jealous colleagues.

Relieved she wasn't on clean-up duty tonight, she headed for the staff closet to grab her jacket. The club was starting to empty. Only a few groups of stragglers remained, split up around the dancefloor, grudgingly moving towards the exit.

"Before you go, Gem, be a gem and check the girl's toilets for us?" One of the large bouncers called. With a rather quieter voice, he continued, "I don't want to go scaring any girls."

Gemma reluctantly agreed.

Before going up the stairs, she walked over to her date for the night: Ethan.

"I'm sorry I just have to do something quickly before I leave."

He gave her a nod. "That's fine. Just make sure you come back." The tall boy standing next to him let out a laugh. Not a joke she was in on.

She hid her quizzical expression and headed upstairs to the toilets. As she reached the top, the club lights turned on signalling time was definitely up for the stragglers.

The smell of mixed perfumes clung to the air and did nothing to mask the smell of vomit. The owner had decorated the toilets lavishly, but after a night of use by drunken women, they were no better than unmaintained, unattended public toilets.

Gemma was glad she didn't drink. Her placement as a trainee nurse in A&E put her off going to nightclubs.

Glad most of the cubicles were empty, she had one left to check: the disabled toilet around the corner. Gemma caught a couple in there once and she had never been so embarrassed.

The room was quiet. She was confident it was empty. Rounding the corner, she was dismayed to see the door closed and the red sticker signalling it was engaged. Holding her breath, she pushed at the door, hoping no one was there.

Oh, no.

It didn't budge. She really didn't want to see another pair at it.

"Come on, guys! Wrap it up. Time to come out. I'll unlock the door in ten seconds." She rapped on the door as confidently as she could. Listening for the sounds of shuffling, she paused. There was nothing but silence.

"Right, make yourself decent. I'm unlocking it." She rattled the handle in warning but nothing happened.

Maybe there's no one in there?

Taking out a hair clip that held a small plait on the side of her head, she undid the lock. The door resisted as she tried to push it open. It was blocked. Something was behind it. Something... or someone.

"Oh crap!" she exclaimed. Were they unconscious?

She pushed harder at the door and whoever was behind it moved enough for her to stick her head through the small gap.

Unable to see due to the angle, she pushed again. She didn't want to injure the person but if they were dying, they wouldn't care if she gave them a bruise.

Using a little more strength, she shoved the door in a final attempt and there came a long groan in reply.

"Thank God!" she exhaled.

A girl laid wrapped around the toilet bowl.

She was alive.

CHAPTER 4

'Well, Ethan boy, another one legged it from you. This one didn't even know you!' Matthew teased, placing his arm over Ethan's shoulder.

"Never mind. Better luck next time." Cam patted Ethan's other shoulder as they waited for Kelly to drag Brooke away from chatting up the bouncers.

Ethan wasn't really bothered about the barmaid he half-heartedly asked out. Cam had already called Jenny. If he knew where she was, he wasn't telling him. Ethan had her number. He would text her and check she was okay tomorrow. He hoped she didn't regret the kiss and leave. She didn't seem to be the type to ditch.

As they headed towards the doors, Cam left the boys to put his arm affectionately over Brooke and Kelly.

"I can't believe Jenny went home," Brooke grumbled.

"You're the last ones standing," Cam assured her.

Ethan smiled weakly. His ego had taken a massive knock but at least it was only him who knew.

"Let's go grab some food?" He suggested as they followed the crowd being ushered into the street.

***

Jenny came round and saw a sweet face looking down at her. Trying her hardest to move, she couldn't. Her legs were as steady as jelly.

Her face flushed with shame as she attempted to speak to the girl trying to help her. The words came out garbled. Apologising profusely in the drunkest way possible, she did all she could to help the girl get her back down the stairs where the bouncers had just finished kicking everyone out.

How is it so late? Where are my friends?

Looking around the empty club like a lost puppy, Jenny felt tears pool in her eyes. If it wasn't for this girl under her arm, she would be truly alone and immobile.

The girl mumbled to the bouncers who watched her dubiously. It seemed to last as long as their journey down the stairs. After a second, they began moving again but this time it was out into the fresh night air.

Stumbling down one step to the pavement, she was grateful the girl kept her upright. They were heading towards the taxi rank. She couldn't hear what the girl was saying – her mind was busy processing everyone moving past her, along with the flashes of light from the traffic on the road. All she could do was concentrate on walking.

Big bronze, bouncy curls suddenly filled her vision.

"Brooooookkeeee!" Jenny groaned, sounding like she spoke through a cardboard tube.

Brooke embraced her and moved under her opposite arm, taking over from the girl. Now being cosseted by her lovely friend, Jenny tried walking with less support but Brooke wasn't so steady.

Only a second passed before Jenny's heel caught in the cobbled street and she toppled. As she fell, she closed her eyes, bracing for impact. Instead of the impact, though, she felt strong arms catch her and they gently turned her upright. Opening her eyes, Jenny saw Ethan looking down at her.

Her vision blurry, she felt more arms surrounding her. Still falling forwards, instead of being upright where she was meant to be, she saw the world go sideways. Ethan and Brooke caught her again. She heard concern in Ethan's voice,

"What the hell? What's happened to her?"

Tired from the concentration, her body surrendered. She flopped over his arm backwards this time, unable to control her movements. Prizing her eyes open, she saw the girl who helped her walking away. She had cute red dolly shoes. It looked like Cam was chasing her.

"Cam!" Jenny tried to call before she passed out. Waking in the taxi, she leaned on Ethan's shoulder, focusing on the smell of his aftershave. Praying to feel less sick and not cause any more trouble, she stayed quiet and listened to the voices around her. They were taking her home.

The smell of greasy kebab infiltrated her nostrils and sick rose to her throat. She let out an involuntary groan and Ethan realised she was awake. He propped her upright.

"Hold it in, Jen. We gotta get you home."

Heaving once, she heard the taxi driver shout. Cam protested the taxi driver's complaints as she heaved once more.

A moment later, the car slowed and Brooke began shouting: "You idiot taxi man. You can't kick her out; she's ill. This taxi stinks anyway!"

Thankfully, her protests seemed to work. The car continued. The first stop had to be Ethan's.

"When I get out, sit here, Jen," he said. "The window's there if you need it."

There was another grumble from the taxi driver and Brooke shouted once more. The warm night air, mixed with the smell of food, curdled her stomach as Ethan got out of the taxi.

Her support now gone, she dived for the pavement, unable to stop the fluids that poured out of her. She saw Ethan jump back from the vomit that almost hit his shoes.

"That's it! Out of the car – now!" The taxi driver shouted.

Jenny heard the driver's door slam and Ethan's shoes disappeared from sight. There were muffled sounds of Ethan and the taxi driver arguing, then an unbearable smell of alcohol. There was vomit everywhere. She was laying in it.

Jenny struggled and crawled so she was completely out of the taxi. Using all her might, she pushed herself up until she stood independently. She heard a pair of feet running towards her, seeing Ethan she beamed but he shot her a worried glance. Then everything went blank again.

CHAPTER 5

Jenny woke. Her vision was blurry and her stomach churned. She had had hangovers before but nothing that ever felt like this. Her eyes fluttered as they tried to take in the light that spilled through the gaps of blue curtains.

Blue curtains? She didn't recognise them.

Panic and the need to move rose through her, but the thumping worsened every time she tried so she stopped in defeat. Closing her eyes, she focused on the noises around her, hoping it would help her figure out where she was.

The room around her was quiet but she could hear a faint sound of birds singing as if it was early morning. Wishing she was still asleep so she didn't have to feel so ill, she forced open her eyes.

Where am I?

There were mirrored wardrobes next to a chest of draws, containing aftershave, an old PlayStation and a small TV. Getting used to moving again, her eyes wandered, looking for more clues.

The walls were white with no posters or pictures. It wasn't Cam's room, and Brooke's room was totally pink. Using all her energy, she pulled herself up to a seated position and held her head.

Is it Ethan's?

On the bedside table on her right, there was a small glass of water and a packet of paracetamols. Presuming they were for her, she fumbled towards them. Her body shivered as the cold air outside of the warm quilt touched her skin.

She hadn't drunk enough to feel this rough. Had she been spiked?

Her mother's friend's daughter ended up in hospital a few weeks earlier after being spiked. *Was it those boys who were chatting up Brooke? Was Brooke okay?*

The thought of her parents made panic rise through her. They would be so worried. Hopefully, Cam would have sorted that. He always looked after her. Was he here?

The room was calm but she needed to get up. Not wanting to make any noise, she pulled back the duvet and swung her legs off the bed. They hovered above the floor.

What if they're squeaky floorboards?

Her head still throbbing, she put slight pressure on the floor and was grateful the thick cushioned carpet minimised the sounds of her movement.

Her bag hung neatly on the back of the bedroom door. Tiptoeing over, she opened it and pulled out her phone. The battery was dead.

Great.

A faint noise of a TV came from outside of the room. Opening the bedroom door, she grimaced at the clicking noise the handle made as it turned. Poking her head through the gap to the landing, she stood waiting and listening.

The TV sound was coming from downstairs. Opposite her, an oak banister stood out against whitewashed walls, trailing down to the ground floor. Cautiously, she crept down the carpeted stairs, trying not to make a sound.

The frizz of her hair rubbed against her face and she didn't want to imagine how her makeup must look. Peering down at her dress, she wished she wore something less revealing last night.

Whose house is this? Where am I?

Getting to the bottom, she set foot into a passageway that led to the front door of the house. Cursing herself under her breath for not bringing her bag downstairs with her, she tried to peer through the frosted glass door to her right. It sounded like the TV was in this room.

Ignoring the throbbing in her head, she leaned in closer to see if it improved her view. Unfortunately, she didn't have time to check properly. She heard footsteps on the other side and the door opened briskly. There stood Ethan.

"Hi," she managed, not knowing what to say

"How are you feeling?" he asked.

She could feel the weight of his stare as he opened the door fully signalling for her to enter into a cosy, small living room. Crossing her arms to cover her chest, she followed him, her mind racing,

"I'm not feeling great. What happened?" Her eyes moved away from him as he looked at her again.

"You were a bit of a mess last night," he said playfully.

"After you were sick, the taxi driver wouldn't let you get back in the car. So, I brought you here."

Looking around the room, she hoped his family wasn't there.

"My parents aren't here, don't worry," he added as if reading her mind, "This is our guest house."

Guest house? On a farm?

Her shoulders relaxed. It was embarrassing enough being in this state. At least it was only Ethan here.

"Did I even drink that much? I don't think I did." Feeling dizzy, Jenny held her head to keep herself steady.

"Have a sit down," Ethan grabbed her and helped lower her onto the deep cushions of the sofa. Her body registered his touch which only made her head spin faster.

"I'll go get you a drink. Do you want water, tea, coffee?"

. "I've troubled you enough. I should be getting home. My parents will be worried."

She tried to get up but struggled against the depths of the cushions, wishing the cushy depths would swallow her up so she could forget about this whole situation. Eventually, she gave up, unable to go anywhere.

"Cam said he would talk to your parents and – no offence – you don't look well enough to go anywhere."

"Thanks" she recoiled.

"I said no offence," he said sportingly.

Unpausing the TV, he asked again: "Water, tea, coffee, squash? Man of variety, me."

"Tea would be lovely, please."

Using her facial muscles caused her head to pound louder. She winced. Ethan was watching but she was in too much pain to care. She felt cold all over.

"Tea it is. Sugar?" Ethan got up and walked towards a door in the room which Jenny assumed led to a kitchen.

"That would be great." She tried to focus on the TV. He was watching an Adam Sandler film.

Hearing the sound of the kettle, she shivered. It reminded her of warmth. Unsure if it was the room or her outfit, she felt frozen.

"Not sure if you wanted to, but did you want to borrow any of my clothes? My sister always pinches my hoodies," Ethan called from the kitchen. She didn't know he had a sister.

"No, I'm okay. Thanks, though," she called back, shivering and regretting the words as they came out of her mouth.

Ethan returned to the room with a brown thick furry blanket, "Here then. Have this in case you get cold".

"Thanks." She took it from him gratefully.

"Where did you sleep?" she asked curiously. She didn't see any other bedroom doors upstairs.

"With the sheep in the barn" he winked, making Jenny grin.

"I can't believe this is my first visit to your farm and I'm a hungover mess." Seeing how fresh and handsome he looked made Jenny want to hide under the blanket. Smiling, Ethan shook his head and returned to the kitchen, leaving her to her thoughts.

Tucking her feet under herself Jenny pulled the blanket over her, covering her entirety. The warmth and background noise of the TV helped her relax. The pounding in her head became rhythmic and she closed her eyes.

***

Ethan ran his fingers through his hair. Having Jenny curled up on his sofa was not how he thought this weekend would pan out. Carrying her last night from the lane to the family's converted barn was an experience.

Grinning, he imagined what he must have looked like trying to carry her through the narrow doors without hitting her head. Ethan looked down at the tea he made and squirmed a little. He never understood the fuss around hot drinks, he hated the idea of them. If Jenny wanted tea, though, that's what he would have, too. Carrying the two pale blue mugs into the living room, he saw her brown hair draped over her face. She was fast asleep under the fluffy blanket.

Black smudges surrounded her eyes but they didn't falter the beautiful shape of her face or how peaceful she looked.

Not sure what to do, he retreated to the kitchen to dispose of the tea. Then he grabbed his jacket. Best head out to see his parents. They didn't seem happy he didn't stay in the house last night. The missed calls were becoming frequent.

Hoping Jenny would wake by the time he returned, he left a note on the table so she knew not to leave.

Just popping to my parents, see you soon! X

He felt silly for adding the kiss but didn't regret it as he closed the kitchen door behind him.

It's what people do on texts, right?

CHAPTER 6

The room was silent when Jenny woke for the second time that day. The TV was turned off and the light in the room was sombre.

How long have I slept?

Sitting up, she listened for Ethan but the silence told her the house was empty.

Realising she was desperate for the toilet, she stood, a little more steady on her feet than before. Wondering where his bathroom could be, she headed to the door that led to the kitchen.

Maybe it's through here.

Peering through the door, she gingerly pressed the light switch, flooding the room with a warm glow. The spotlights on the ceiling revealed a pristine, white kitchen and granite counters.

Noticing two empty mugs sitting on the kitchen counter as she moved, she tipped toed to an internal door at the back of the room. On the other side, the welcoming smell of soap and aftershave tingled her nostrils.

The fan whirred as she pulled the light cord. Gently closing the door behind her, she took in the room that was pale blue and decorated with seashells. The door clicked shut and her body visibly relaxed.

After relieving herself, she was dismayed to see her reflection in the mirror above the bathroom sink.

Ethan saw me like this?

The foundation had rubbed off her skin and she could most definitely pass for a panda. Splashing water in her face, she appreciated its warmth until she heard what sounded like a front door opening. She froze.

"Jen, you here?" Ethan called.

"Just in your bathroom! Won't be a minute," she replied, fumbling to turn off the tap.

Rushing, she grabbed toilet paper to dry her face. She didn't want to leave evidence of her panda eyes all over the crisp white hand towel that hung next to the sink.

Hearing footsteps in the kitchen, she pulled down her dress as far as it could go, without revealing her chest too much. She stepped out of the bathroom feeling embarrassed. Ethan stood there in a padded wax jacket. His hair was wet from the rain. He gave her a curious look.

"Sorry, I hope you don't mind me using your bathroom." She cringed and wiped the underneath of her eyes again in case any residue remained.

"No, course not. Sorry I took longer than planned. I came back earlier but you were still asleep."

Jenny remembered the TV being turned off.

"Cam rang me," Ethan began. "He couldn't get hold of you. Your parents think you're at Brooke's house but you'll have to use your key. They've gone to Cardiff overnight."

Amid her state and the new surroundings, she had forgotten about her parents' night away. She raised her hand to her mouth in shock.

"I didn't take my keys last night – and my phone's dead." She winced and rolled her eyes at herself. "I'm hopeless. How could I forget?"

Ethan laughed. "Don't worry. I didn't see your keys when I dropped your bag last night. I cleared it with my parents. They're fine with you staying here… If you want to, that is?" He paused. "My sister lent you some clothes, too. The bags in the living room if you want them." He leaned against the kitchen counter, hands in his pockets, awaiting her response. When she didn't answer right away, he added, "I can give you a lift to Brook's or Cam's if you'd rather?"

Suddenly aware of the suspense she was creating, Jenny replied without thinking: "Will you stay here with me? It's a guest house, you said."

He smirked.

"If you want me to, yeah. I just have to finish helping my dad. It should only take ten minutes."

Jenny couldn't believe how brazen she had been.

"Only our family and friends ever stay here," Ethan explained. "It's almost always empty."

Reassured, she let her body relax.

"Thank you. I don't think I could face questions from Cam or Brooke right now."

He grinned, understanding the questions she might want to avoid.

"It's okay. I think the spare charger may fit your phone, by the way." Pulling out the middle kitchen drawer, he retrieved a lead. "This your slot?"

She moved closer to see. It was the right one. The proximity to him made her feel giddy.

"That's perfect, thanks," she said as he handed her the lead. For a moment, their hands touched.

"Feel free to make yourself at home. Whatever you need just let me know." He looked into her eyes but his hand didn't let go of the lead. She found herself staring at his lips. She could imagine how good it would be to kiss him. Timidly, though, she pulled the lead from his hand and stepped back.

"Your sister is kind. I can't thank you enough." The air felt tight, locking them in the moment. Unable to look away, she broke the intensity by softly muttering, "You better go help your dad if he's waiting."

Ethan's eyes danced with amusement.

"I best had." Still smiling, he backed out of the room, leaving her wishing he didn't actually go.

Feeling human after a shower, Jenny pulled on the clothes Ethan's sister had loaned her. Grateful to be out of her dress, she dismissed the embarrassment of having to borrow them in the first place. She observed herself in the mirror. The grey jogging bottoms fit perfectly but the top was a little tight, causing it to rise above her waist.

It'll have to do, she thought.

Before Ethan returned she put her phone on charge and stood in the bedroom, holding it, pressing the power button, willing for it to come alive. It powered on, and when the main screen came to life, she saw a notification,

From Cam:
Be careful Jen, I mean it. x

Hearing the front door open, she placed her phone on the windowsill. What did that mean? She would call Cam later to ask.

Ethan was at the kitchen counter emptying a brown paper bag. He looked up at her as she entered.

"My mother's given me food to cook for us."

Jenny raised her eyebrows in surprise.

He can cook?

"I'm quite hungry but you don't look pleased about cooking…"

Watching his puzzled face as he emptied the contents of the bag, she grinned. "Want me to cook?"

He slid ingredients over the kitchen counter to her and looked relieved. "I was hoping you would offer. I can't cook an egg to save my life."

She tutted playfully.

"Are these from the chickens on the farm?" The idea of eating food from the farm was fascinating.

"No, they're eggs from the city. Had them delivered especially." At first she couldn't tell if he was serious. When he laughed, though, she know it was a joke.

"Haha," she exaggerated, nudging him with her elbow. "I always wondered what it would be like to live on a farm. Is it like how you see it on TV?"

Ethan shrugged. "I guess so. A lot harder than it looks on TV, mind you. You don't see the rain, the mud, the animals going off to slaughter." Seeing her eyes widen, he backtracked. "We do all sorts. So it's always busy."

He ended with a grin and Jenny responded in kind, not wanting his slipup to dampen the mood. Not quite knowing what to say, she picked up the egg carton and looked inside it. Most of the eggs still had feathers attached to them.

"They might need a wash." He nodded towards the sink while putting bread in the toaster.

"We're only cracking them," she explained. "Where's your frying pan?"

"In here." He leaned over her to reach the cupboard door above her head. Then he pulled a heavy-looking frying pan over her shoulder. The smell of his aftershave lingered. "Sorry."

"No worries." She lowered her gaze. "Are you sure you don't mind me staying the night? Your sofa is super comfy. I feel a lot better after that sleep."

This time, he looked at her with surprise.

"Of course I don't mind. It's fine. You can take the bedroom again."

"No, you've done too much for me already," she protested.

"Maybe I want to," he responded, watching her cheeks blush. "So, last night do you remember going to the toilets before we lost you?" Ethan eyed her.

Jenny racked her brains, trying to remember. "You lost me?" She moved over to the hob. "I remember being on the dancefloor, we were dancing. It's all a bit fuzzy from there."

Cracking the eggs open in the hot pan, she tried to ignore him watching her.

"I have no idea what happened. Do you?"

Ethan only shrugged. "I followed to check you were okay. Then you kissed me."

Jenny's body went rigid.

"We kissed?!"

Busying himself, Ethan opened a tin of baked beans on the opposite counter, continuing as if they were having a normal conversation.

"I didn't see you again till we found you being helped to the taxi rank by a barmaid." His voice was casual. Matter-of-fact.

"The girl with the red shoes?" A memory of red dolly shoes come back to her.

Ethan laughed before holding his chest, gesturing he was wounded. "You remember a stranger's shoes and not our kiss?"

Noting the way he said "our kiss," Jenny smirked.

"It couldn't have been anything special if I don't remember it," she teased.

She turned to face him, her back now to the stove. At the same time, he moved towards her and she steadied herself. The butterflies in her stomach were flying wild. Holding the pan of baked beans, he walked to where she stood. Now in front of her, he reached behind her back, placing down the pan and turning down the flame on the hob.

"Want to retract that statement?"

He stared at her, waiting for a response. Her skin came alive with goosebumps as her eyes dared him to kiss her, again. Thankfully, he did. Wrapping his arms around her waist, he spun her away from the stove and his warm lips met hers.

She didn't have a chance to take a breath. Her eyes closed and the feeling of desire burned through her. Consuming him like oxygen in return, she heard him let out a soft moan as she nipped his bottom lip. Effortlessly, he lifted her onto the counter. Her legs wrapped around his body instinctively as his hunger turned to her neck.

At that moment, a voice called from the front door. It opened and, in a split second, they parted. Her heart raced, she jumped down off the counter and Ethan tried to control his panting.

"My sister," he breathed.

A girl who looked a year or two younger than Jenny strode into the kitchen. "You must be Jenny?" She asked, "Mam forgot to pack you dessert so made me walk all the way here. You owe me!" She placed the brown paper bag she held down on the counter.

Turning her attention to the eggs sputtering and burning in the frying pan, Emma looked at her brother and the girl with flushed cheeks. "Your eggs are burning but I'm glad the clothes fit. I'll be off." She headed through the kitchen door as quickly as she came.

"Oh and be safe, you two." They heard her call from the passage.

"Bye, Emma," Ethan called in a condescending tone.

They heard the front door close and their eyes danced as they looked at one another. "Well, that was... ahh... yeah." Ethan grinned before they both burst out laughing. Walking over to the hob, he turned it off. "How about I get us a takeaway instead?"

Jenny held a hand to her cheeks which must have been glowing red.

"Sounds like a plan," she said. "I'll come, too, for some cool air." He grinned and walked to her, gently wrapping his arms around her waist. Pulling her close to him, this time he planted a lingering kiss on her forehead.

"Come on, let's go."

He grabbed his hoodie off the back of a kitchen chair and handed it to her. Accepting it, she followed him back through the house, her mind whirring in an effort to keep up with her thoughts, or lack thereof.

CHAPTER 7

(Two Weeks Later)

Working for a company that had offices in a business complex was epic. A free canteen, TV at lunch. With one week left in training, Jenny was going to make the most of it. Then it would be back to sandwiches and the same old teacher gossip.

Carrying her tray of food, she shifted her weight. Her bag hung awkwardly from her shoulder and her phone was ringing.

"Really?" she huffed, trying to adjust her arm to prevent her handbag from sliding off altogether. The last thing she needed was for everything to crash to the floor in the middle of the canteen.

"Honestly," she proclaimed, taking a seat opposite Ashleigh her new work friend, "If anything else goes wrong today!"

Setting down the tray of food on the table, Jenny rummaged in her bag. Her phone had stopped ringing but she had a text from Ethan. Her face lit up.

"Your Prince Charming calling you?" Ashleigh teased. "How inconvenient."

After finishing texting Ethan back Jenny, put her phone away.

"Me and Eth are going on a double date tonight with our friends Matthew and Kelly. Ethan's a little gutted.

Ashleigh stared at her, waiting for her to elaborate.

"We're going to a new restaurant. Ethan hates fine dining."

Tucking into her food for a second, she paused. Ashleigh wasn't eating again, just drinking her usual black coffee. Jenny shook her head.

"You should eat. Have some food with me? Go on, have a chip," she encouraged, but Ashleigh shook her head. Her blonde fishtail plait brushed her shoulder as she did so.

"I do eat," said Ashleigh, trying not to stare at Jenny's food. "I only have a couple more pounds to lose then I promise I'll eat lunch with you."

Not wanting to push any further, Jenny nodded. "Okay. You're missing out, though. They're delicious."

Walking into the training room, Jenny was greeted with smiling faces. Glancing back, she saw Ashleigh's eyes drop to the floor. She didn't acknowledge anyone.

Taking a seat next to one of the other team members Brie, Jenny shuffled her chair, making it easier for Ashleigh to fit her own onto the end of the table next to her.

"Where were you today, Brie? Didn't see you at lunch," Jenny queried.

Brie knocked on the empty tub sitting on the desk in front of her. "Stayed here today. Salad – bleh."

"Ashleigh's on a diet, too." Jenny leaned back in her seat so Brie and Ashleigh could acknowledge each other.

"That's cool," said Brie. "Maybe we could help each other stay on track. What diet are you on?"

"I'm fasting and doing a ketosis diet," Ashleigh stated before adding, "What one are you doing?"

Brie looked puzzled. "Never heard of a ketosis diet. Sounds serious. Maybe you could tell me about it after training? I'm just calorie counting at the moment."

Jenny spotted Brie's eyes move to Sam, the training manager who had just entered the room. Distracted now, Ashleigh also looked his way, before whispering, "Yeah sure."

Jenny felt a little buzz, maybe she would succeed in getting Ashleigh to make new friends after all.

"Ok let's talk about gaps," Sam began, ignoring the sound of everyone clearing the tables, hiding remnants of food and mobile phones. "It's winter, the door is ajar and there is a draft coming into the room. You are trying to keep the room warm. What do you do?"

"Close it?" Brie answered with confidence. The rest of the group chuckled.

"That's right. You close it," Sam agreed, smiling as he paced back and forth, the table laid out in a single row. "We close the gap to reach our objective of heating the room." He paused, ensuring all eyes were on him. "How about this? A child is struggling with the concept of multiplication. What do you do?"

The room was silent for a little longer but John who was also new answered hesitantly: "Teach them multiplication?"

Replying with a simple "hmm," Sam sauntered to the end of the room and perched himself on the windowsill.

"When it comes to learning, the gap you need to close to reach your objective is harder to identify. If children have gaps in their knowledge, it will be difficult for them to grasp new concepts." He took a breath, his eyes moving along the table, looking at each of them. "If a child cannot count in sequence, how can they learn multiplication?"

Jenny looked around and saw everyone's brains were working just as hard as hers.

"To achieve your goal and teach new concepts, you have to find and close the knowledge gaps. To retain the heat in the room, you have to close the door…" Smiling, he tapped the pile of papers next to him, got up and started handing out booklets. "This is where we intervene and close those gaps. You will be doing what teachers do: assess, plan and record the children's progress. But, unlike teachers, you will have the time to ensure you identify gaps, no matter how small. This is where you make a difference."

There was a rustle of papers as the group began looking through the assessment booklet.

Jenny thought about the children she had worked with. She could imagine how many gaps they might have that hadn't been identified. Smiling, she looked up at Sam. She couldn't wait to get started.

***

Walking out of the restaurant, Ethan acknowledged Jenny with a nod. He grinned ear to ear and rested his arm over her shoulders. In return, she wrapped her arm around his waist. As they stood waiting for Matthew and Kelly, he couldn't help himself. Moving to hold both of her hands, he stood, taking in every detail of her, making her giggle.

"You are the most beautiful girl." He pulled her to his chest. She smelled of soap and felt warm as she nuzzled into him. It was comforting in the cool night air. He held her tightly and she relaxed into him. He heard her take a deep breath.

When the bell above the restaurant door jingled, both of their heads turned and they watched Matthew and Kelly join them on the pavement. The glow from the restaurant disappeared as the door closed behind them.

"You two are so cute together!" Kelly cooed.

"It's nice to have some decent company for a double date, that's for sure," Matthew added.

Ethan didn't need to say anything – just held Jenny's hand as they strolled back to the car park. They were ready to go home.

"So, where's Cam tonight?" Matthew asked Kelly.

No one had seen him for a while.

"I think he's seeing someone. He's being very secretive," she divulged.

"Has he told you anything?" Kelly turned to look at Jenny who shook her head.

"He's been unusually quiet lately."

Ethan watched concern flash across Jenny's face as she spoke. It had been nice to have her all to himself the past two weeks. Ethan knew her and Cam were just friends but that didn't mean her attention wasn't divided when he was around. Hopefully, whatever Cam was up to would keep him busy for a good while.

CHAPTER 8

Concentrating on the beam of the headlights that bounced off the hedges as they drove through the narrow lanes to the farm, Jenny couldn't stop her leg from bouncing.

"You okay?" Ethan asked, resting his hand on her leg, it was reassuring. Jenny glanced at him nervously, and he added, "My parents can't wait to meet you."

"I'm looking forward to meeting them, too." She placed her hand on top of his.

Thinking back to the first night they spent at the guest house on his family farm, and the many nights after it, Jenny's cheeks felt hot. Up until now, they had taken advantage of the vacant house. It was now something Jenny regretted, as her visits without meeting his parents must have left a poor impression. But she couldn't change that now.

Forcing a smile, she gulped as they reached the driveway of the main house. The drive had a mini-island in the middle you could drive around, leaving just enough room to stop at the entrance of the grand-looking home. The guest house was luxurious compared to Jenny's semi-detached terrace, but it was basic compared to the farmhouse. That was beautiful, in a rustic way.

Wow

Opening the large wooden door to the house with his key, Ethan's hand trembled.

Is he nervous, too?

As she followed him inside, warmth and the smell of furniture polish greeted them, mingled with a hint of smoke from a log burner. Ethan rolled his eyes at the sound of footsteps above them.

"My sister coming to cause mischief."

"Hi, Jenny! Nice to finally, formally meet you," Jenny saw Ethan's sister appear at the top of the stairs. Her ginger hair was tied back, revealing brown freckles that dotted her face. Bounding down the stairs, she hung off the bottom banister before calling back up the stairs. "Bryce! Come meet Ethan's girlfriend!"

Jenny's cheeks reddened and Ethan grimaced at how cringe-worthy his sister was being.

"Shush, Emma. Let the poor girl come in." Ethan's mother appeared from the large living area beyond the stairs.

"Come on in, love." Her voice was soft and welcoming. "I'm Alison." she introduced herself and Jenny's tense body relaxed. Together, they led her through to the living area where she could see embers glowing in the hearth. A TV was on in the corner of the room.

"Dad's watching TV in the kitchen. You know what he's like with his documentaries." Alison tutted, smiling as she gestured for them to sit down. "Just watching my soaps. Do you watch them, Jenny?"

"I, err – "

" – Ethan, take Jenny's coat so she can get comfy," Alison instructed. Ethan stood and took her coat back out into the hall. Then his mother continued, "Sorry, love. You were saying…?"

"I don't watch soaps, sorry," Jenny answered. "I used to watch them with my mother but kind of stopped."

"No need to apologise," his mother chuckled. "It's always the same old dramas anyway." She sat in the opposite chair to Jenny and, returning, Ethan relaxed into the seat next to her. The corners of Alison's mouth rose as she watched him reach for Jenny's hand.

"Sorry about Emma. She's a wild one. Takes after my dad," Ethan said. He played with Jenny's fingers as he spoke.

"She's so cheeky," his mother agreed. "Definitely gets it from your dad." Her eyes met Jenny's. Ethan's mother was nothing like Jenny pictured.

She always pictured a farmer's wife to be like the nursery rhyme books she read as a child: plump with a bun on the top of their head. Ethan's mother was much different. She had highlights running through her short, blonde hair. She was trim, too. Jenny could see that Ethan inherited his long thick eyelashes from her.

"How was the meal?" his mother asked, prompting conversation. "I'm impressed you got Ethan out of his muddy wellies to go to a nice place to eat. He'd live on takeaway pizza if he could."

"Beats your cooking," Ethan said with a smirk.

"There's nothing wrong with my cooking, thank you. We might have to get your dad to cook if you think there is." She winked at Jenny. "Please no!" Emma begged, hearing the conversation as she entered the room. "Bryce said he'll be down in a bit. Busy with some game." She raised a brow at Jenny and Ethan holding hands on the double sofa. "You two are getting serious then, eh?"

Ethan looked at Jenny whose cheeks were turning pink again.

"Well, I think that's enough meet and greet. Should we go to my room?" Ethan stood.

"Yeah, sure." Jenny said. Beginning to feel more comfortable with his mother and sister, she rose to follow him.

"You'd better say hello to your father first." his mother ordered.

"Yeah, we can grab some drinks anyway." Ethan called over his shoulder as he led Jenny to an arched door to the kitchen.

"No drinking my Lucozade," Emma called after them.

The kitchen was large and well lived in. There was a backdoor to the left, and wooden counters surrounded most of the walls in the large room. The far wall housed a large Aga. Wood made up the majority of the services, including the island where Ethan's dad was sitting, watching a TV that rested on the counter opposite him.

Looking around, Jenny admired how the decorative dishes, horseshoes and farm animal ornaments made the space feel homely. On the wall behind them was a photo of their family standing in front of a haystack, all of them smiling and happy.

Emma and his younger brother looked alike.
Are Emma and Bryce twins?

Bryce had ginger hair and a freckled face just like Emma. It was the first time she had seen him. They were almost identical.

Ethan cleared his throat.

"Hi, Dad. This is Jenny."

His dad who looked too broad to be comfortable sitting on the thin wooden kitchen stool looked over at them and his face brightened.

"Hello, Jenny! I'm Norman." He got up from the stool and gestured to shake Jenny's hand.

"Ain't you a beaut? What are you doing with this waster?" He winked before tapping Ethan on the shoulder.

"You okay, my boy? How was your meal? Any good?" His dad returned to the stool.

"Yeah, Dad, it was good. What are you watching?" Norman nodded at the TV.

"Just another farming documentary. These fools have no clue, do they? Free to join me."

Ethan stopped and glanced at the screen before grabbing two glasses from the mullioned cupboard above the TV.

"No thanks, Dad. Just grabbing drinks and we're heading on up."

Norman shrugged. "Suit yourselves. Nice to meet you, Jenny." As Ethan poured them water, Norman looked at Jenny. "Are you joining us for breakfast tomorrow? It's early at 6.00 am – sit down, nice fresh eggs from the girls out back."

She nodded. "I'd love to. I have to be up for work anyway so it suits me perfectly." She saw Ethan grinning in the corner of her eye.

"A working girl too, eh," his dad mused.

"You're a lucky boy if she works as hard as your mother, Eth. I won't keep you. Off you go, both."

Ethan glanced back at the TV that now had Norman's full attention again.

"Goodnight, Dad. See you in the morning."

"Eth," his mother called as they headed up the stairs. "If Jenny wants warm feet in the morning, leave her socks on the landing."

Ethan laughed at Jenny's quizzical expression.

"Mam puts our socks over the Aga in the morning to warm them for breakfast. Sounds silly but that stone floor is cold."

He explained as he led her up the stairs. They both let out a breath when Ethan closed his bedroom door. His room was painted blue with blue curtains and oak wardrobes with blue doors.

"I'm going to guess your favourite colour," Jenny teased as Ethan placed their drinks on a desk to the side of his bed.

"Come here." He pulled her to him and kissed her.

Looking up at him, her eyes glistened.

"Your family are lovely."

He moved her onto the bed, his hand behind her head as it fell onto the soft pillow.

"Not as lovely as you." He kissed her again and moved to lay next to her. "Anyway, they can be a bit much."

She turned to face him, leaning on her elbow. "I haven't run yet."

She fluttered her lashes, wanting him to kiss her again. Studying his face, she noted how he wrinkled his nose, making her giggle.

"Sounds perfect." Placing his arm around her, he pulled her body closer to his. "Sorry about my brother not coming to meet you, by the way. Worker by day, gamer by night. That's what he says to get away with being antisocial."

Jenny laughed. "Don't worry. I can meet him at breakfast." She kissed him on the mouth and let it linger before pulling away.

"Mmm," he moaned.

"Oh, before I forget to ask, are Bryce and Emma twins? They look so alike from the picture in the kitchen."

"They are, they were the bane of my life growing up, they always outnumbered me. Still do."

Jenny nodded, she didn't have siblings but she could imagine it would be nice. Sitting up to observe his room, she spotted a red wood acoustic guitar hung on the wall.

"You play the guitar?" He looked at her sheepishly. So, she added, "You have to play me something!"

He bit his bottom lip.

"Please," she pleaded.

Getting up, he plucked it from the wall.

"I'm not singing, though."

He began to play and the longer he continued, the more the crimson colour of his cheeks faded to his natural skin tone.

She listened and watched as his fingers moved up and down the fretboard, playing a slow bewitching melody. Giving a clap of appreciation as he finished, Jenny thought how lucky she was.

"And I thought you couldn't get any more attractive," she joked, the muscle in his arm flexed as he reached to return the guitar to the wall stand and she decided it definitely wasn't a joke.

When he was finished, he turned to her. His eyes were filled with lust.

"I think I'm more than attracted to you, Jen."

He positioned himself on top of her. Taking in the sincere expression on his face, Jenny swallowed the lump forming in her throat. As he planted gentle kisses along her neck and jawline, she closed her eyes, revelling in the pleasure.

He stopped and she opened her eyes to see him staring down at her

"I love you, Jenny Griffiths."

Tears shimmered in her eyes as she rose to kiss him. She couldn't believe he had said it. Said the three words that had been stuck in her mind for the past week. The time they had spent together had been short. After years of knowing each other as friends, it was bizarre – them laying there – but it felt right. More than right.

It felt perfect.

She rose to meet his lips again. Her eyes closed.

"I love you, too," she whispered.

CHAPTER 9

Cam entered his bedroom and found Gemma inspecting his photo of a young boy smiling. Realising he was standing there, she looked up and observed him in return.

"That's my dad," he said. It was the only picture he had of his father.

"You look alike."

Cam did think he looked similar.

"My mam would love to disagree with you on that one."

Gemma smirked. "Well, I don't want to disagree with your mum the first time we meet."

She placed the photo back on his bedside table.

"He's currently in South America somewhere..." Cam offered. "Left when we were about five. Mam took it hard. All the pictures went, except that one I kept."

***

Gemma patted the space on the bed next to her, indicating for Cam to sit.

"So, do you stay in touch?" This was the first time he had talked about his dad.

"We speak every now and then, but I never really talk about him. It's easier not to." His voice trailed off.

Placing her hand on his arm, she gave it a reassuring squeeze.

"Whenever you want to talk about him, I'm happy to listen."

Cam looked like a giant in his bedroom. It baffled her how he still fit into the single bed. She half-expected his feet would hang off the end. His room was painted red – her favourite colour.

Remnants of his childhood remained; a Manchester United poster on the wall, a Star Wars Lego set on top of his wardrobe.

She stood and turned to look out of the window above his bed. The view of the valley expanding outwards from his headboard was quite breathtaking.

Cam rose and stood behind her, his arms wrapped around her waist. He rested his head on her shoulder.

"When is your mother and sister home again?" she asked, chewing the edge of her fingernail. She hadn't got to meet Kelly the night she found the girl passed out in the toilets. The girl who she now knows to be called Jenny.

"Won't be long," he replied before taking hold of her arms to stop the nail biting. She always did it when she was nervous. They had been in their own perfect little bubble over the last month and now she was meeting his family. "They usually close the shop early on Fridays unless they are swamped."

Gemma nodded.

"You know we could have just stayed here for dinner. You didn't have to book a fancy place."

Cam grinned, "The business is taking off and I'm flying the nest. I want to celebrate."

Let's just hope your mother likes me. Gemma thought, staring out the window. She could get used to a view of these mountains.

CHAPTER 10

The introductions went better than Cam thought they would.

Gemma was a hard person to dislike. Her and Kelly clicked instantly, bonding over the same brand of makeup they wore. Cam appreciated she didn't bring up that Gemma was the girl Ethan was going to take home on their last night out together.

He watched his mother Maria as she sat smiling in adoration as the girls chatted before she looked at him.

The taxi was on time and the four of them got to the restaurant at 07:00 pm sharp.

"So, why couldn't Matthew join us again?" Cam asked his sister as they approached the manor house. It wasn't like Matthew to miss out on eating.

Kelly painted on a feigned smile. "He's had to take his mother shopping. She needed a new dress or something" She trailed off and Cam detected a forlorn tone in her voice.

Is Kelly worried about Matthew?

Picking the conversation back up, Gemma chimed in, "I can't wait to meet him. He sounds fun. You both seem to make a great couple from what Cam's told me."

Taking in Gemma's assurances, Cam saw his sister's shoulders relax. *Has Matthew been acting strange lately?* He racked his brains. Since his increase in workload, he hadn't really spoken with Matthew or even noticed if he'd been quiet.

They entered the large doorways of Brenhinol house, manor hotel with a top-rated restaurant on the outskirts of the valley. Having only been here with clients last week, Cam navigated through the reception and veered right, towards the terrace restaurant.

It was too cold to use the terrace for alfresco dining in the winter but the recently installed floor-to-ceiling windows afforded diners a spectacular panoramic view from inside.

Cam was excited to see that view again. The valley unfolded before them with streetlamps creating a river of light that flowed through the sloped mountainsides. It reminded him of the nights he and Jenny would watch the lights turn on from the hill brow of their street. Happy memories.

The Maître d' appeared and greeted them at his station. Cam spotted Maria smoothing over her burgundy dress in the corner of his eye. She looked beautiful. He couldn't remember the last time he saw her wear a dress.

Leading them to the far side of the restaurant, the Maître d' indicated their front row seats, next to the towering glass. As they approached, the windows reflected the lights and scenes of the restaurant straight back at them. All three women used the opportunity to check their hair in the reflection.

"Those reflections are prettier than the view," he said.

Maria tutted and Kelly pretended to gag. Though, Gemma's eyes met his. Hers were full of laughter.

"So, what's all this for then, my dear boy?" Maria queried, a curious expression on her face.

"I'm surprised you didn't invite Jenny and Ethan?" Kelly wondered out loud. "This place is very nice." She eyed the elegant room again.

"I did check with them, actually," Cam shrugged.

"Yeah, I thought you hadn't seen them in a while…"

Cam didn't rise to Kelly's bait. She knew Ethan asked Gemma out before he did. Instead, he just watched his sister help herself to the lemon water sitting on the table between them.

"They had plans but I'll be seeing them tomorrow with Ethan playing in the pub," he explained. "Are you and Matthew going?"

"Yes, of course. Matthew is basically Ethan's roadie. Helps him set up and carry stuff. He loves it."

Not detecting anything off in her voice when she mentioned Matthew, Cam made a mental note to give him a ring in the morning. It was hard when he found out his sister and his best friend got together all those years ago. Now that their relationship was years down the line, it put him on edge not knowing which direction it could go.

"I'm sorry I can't come tomorrow and meet everyone," Gemma declared, biting her lip. "They're really short-staffed at work. I just couldn't let them down."

Cam placed his hand on her knee and his mother turned to Gemma.

"Yes, Cam told us you're a nurse. You're still in training?"

Gemma nodded. "I do some bar work for extra money. I'm not able to work daytimes with my bursary and placement in A&E. But another year and I'm hoping to be qualified."

"How's your business going?" Gemma asked.

Cam had told her about the shop his mother and Kelly opened, making bespoke dresses. It was doing well, especially with all the winter balls the local schools had decided to host this year. He was glad she brought it up. It would go in their favour.

"It's going great," said Cam's mother. "We're just hoping to keep up the momentum. Get ourselves recognised. Kelly's the star of the show though, I just help."

Kelly blushed as Gemma turned to look at her.

When the waiter assigned to their table took their orders, Cam's mother spoke again: "You avoided my question, Cameron. What's all this about?"

He gave her a mischievous look, the same one he used to give her as a little boy.

"So, uh, just wanted to break some news really, and celebrate."

Kelly and Maria gave him their full attention, which he hated.

"So… the business is doing well. Me and Jack landed some pretty big clients here last week." The corners of his mouth rose as he spoke about the deals with his business partner. He took a breath before continuing. "I'm going to be spending most of my time in the city working with Jack. So…" Gemma's hand tightened around his, which still rested on her knee, "I've decided – no, *we've* decided," he corrected himself, "that it's the right time to move out. Gemma and I will be moving in together. Closer to work." Just before words could escape his mother's mouth, he jumped in again. "Gemma's commute to the hospital is a nightmare and we're looking at renting closer."

"I'm spending a fortune on petrol and parking," she explained. "Two birds, one stone, all that."

At that moment, the waiter brought their drinks and Cam busied himself with pleasantries, all too aware that Kelly and his mother remained silent.

"Moving out?" his mother finally said when the waiter departed. "Well, that's a bit of a shock. Are you sure? You're both still young."

Maria's face was kind but her tone had caution attached. Cam expected her to take it hard but he wanted her to see it as a good thing.

"I know it sounds soon…" Gemma spoke before he could. "But we're happy and we'll be doing it sensibly; renting, splitting all the costs in half. It's purely transactional with the added benefit of spending more time together. It's a win-win."

Cam saw his mother's eye twitch as Gemma used the word home in reference to him. Kelly appeared paralysed. They didn't speak often but he knew she liked having around. He could almost hear her thoughts.

Who would catch the spiders and change the light bulbs? Not wanting to cause them any more shock, Cam didn't mention they had already viewed a house and paid a deposit.

"Congratulations, both, then." Maria raised her glass that was already almost empty. "This'll be a night we remember. And well done on the big clients. I can't wait to hear about them."

Cam lifted his pint and took his first sip. It didn't taste as good as he hoped it would. He was grateful for his mother's gracious response, though, however sincere.

CHAPTER 11

As his brown leather shoes clapped against the pavement, Cam tried to let the sound of the river that ran alongside him fill his ears. With cars passing him on his right and the river rushing down the valley to his left, it should have been enough external stimulation to distract him from his thoughts.

As much as he had missed her, Cam had managed to avoid seeing Jenny since she had got with Ethan. He frowned. Jenny had been charmed. She was happy, Ethan was happy, but the elephant Cam carried was far too big for the room he was about to enter.

He was sure Jenny didn't know that when she disappeared on their last night out, Ethan wasted no time in asking Gemma to go home with him. Gemma who he was now moving in with. He felt guilty for not telling Jenny that Ethan shouldn't be trusted and he was still torn.

Should I have told her? Should I tell her now? Am I just being over protective?

Knowing that Ethan had Gemma's interest first had left Cam bruised. He remembered spending all night trying to get her attention from the other side of the bar. When Gemma turned up outside the club with Jenny under her arm, Ethan disregarded her so Cam took his opportunity. He was extremely thankful things turned out the way they did, if Gemma didn't find Jenny and bump back into them, she might have gone home with Ethan that night. His body shuddered at the thought.

As much as he wanted to, he couldn't avoid going to Ethan's gig tonight. Everyone was beginning to wonder why he was being so distant and he needed to break the news that he would be moving, and who he was moving in with.

Two birds, one stone.

Cam's palms were sweating, The Sherwood Inn, the pub that Ethan was playing at that night, was now in sight. Nestled underneath a large bowstring bridge that crossed over a river on the opposite side of the road, its warm lights emanated from the pub windows. Fairy lights strung just below the guttering created a welcoming glow in the gloom of the winter evening.

His hand slipped down the brass handle as he took a breath and pulled open the door.

On entering The Sherwood Inn, he lingered near a second doorway on his left that led to a lounge. Inside, older men nursed their pints and mumbled in companionable musings. A door on his right, meanwhile, led to a bar that was empty throughout the week but packed on weekends.

Cam headed through the door on the right. Its hinges squeaked in protest and faces looked up at him as he entered. He didn't recognise any of them.

Knowing the gang would be in their usual spot towards the back, tucked behind a pillar, he headed for the bar.

"Double Jack and Coke, please."

Managing to avoid Jenny and Ethan as a couple had been tricky. Now it was show time.

Waiting for his drink, he turned to examine the long room. It hadn't changed since they were teenagers. Their spot behind the pillar was ideal for sneaking in their own drinks. At the back there was a makeshift stage.

That's new.

It was still hard to fathom Ethan played music, let alone to a crowd. Moving his eyes to their usual spot at the table that had a bench and stools instead of normal seats. He could just about see the back of Matthew's blond, spiky head. He saw Kelly sitting opposite him and assumed the others were just out of sight behind the pillar.

Drink in hand, he made his way towards the table through the narrow pathway of pulled-out chairs and bodies that stood drinking and chatting.

The rest of the group came into sight, Ethan was sitting next to Kelly with Brooke on his right.

Where's Jenny?

He sucked in his ribs and turned sidewards to squeeze through a narrow gap between the backs of two occupied chairs. As he breathed out, he felt a hand touch his arm.

"Sorry." He turned to apologise but Jenny stood there beaming up at him.

"Hello, Stranger. Long time, no see!" Twisting, she slotted through the narrow gap after him and giggled as she embraced him. "We've missed you."

His worries about upsetting her melted away as they hugged. Jenny was the most understanding, kindest and naive person he knew. If Ethan was as good to her as she made out, he wouldn't need to worry about Ethan's short attention span when it came to women. He would just look out for her like he always had.

"We're in the usual spot." Jenny overtook him through a small gap on their right and he followed her to the table where everyone looked on at them, waving.

"The lone wolf returns!" Matthew rose and he howled, making fellow drinkers turn their heads in amusement.

They slapped hands in greeting and lent in for a bro hug before Cam took a seat next to Matthew on the shortest stool ever. Jenny sat on the stool to Cam's right, opposite Brooke.

"Not a lone wolf anymore," Kelly teased.

"So, you've filled them in?" he questioned his sister. She shook her head

"All on you, brother." Her smiley face softened before turning wistful. It had been a quiet taxi ride home the night before.

"Wasn't you bringing a girl here for us to meet?" Ethan asked, looking at him, then Jenny, then back at him again. Cam smirked and raised his eyebrow.

Was Ethan becoming territorial?

The gang took the news that he was moving from the Valleys better than he expected. Jenny was upset that she didn't have an inclination he might move away but he had been absent so long the others had guessed already.

When he told them about Gemma, the barmaid he met the night Jenny got wasted, he saw Ethan make the link.

"Is that the girl that found Jenny in the toilets?" he interrupted.

"Yeah," Cam replied, smoothing over the question before turning to Jenny. "Lucky you did drink too much. I asked her for her number when she returned you."

Ethan didn't say any more but Jenny got quite excited

"No way?! The girl with the red shoes? You're moving in with the girl with red shoes?"

Cam grinned. "She does wear red shoes, yeah. How did you know?"

Jenny laughed. "It's the one thing I do remembered from that night, I never thought I'd meet my hero. Yay!"

A barman approaching the table interrupted the conversation, letting Ethan know he was due on stage in five minutes.

"Come on, Jen. You gotta do the 'oos' for me!" Ethan encouraged.

"Don't be silly! No!"

The others looked at them curiously.

"She added some 'oooh' sounds to one of my songs," he explained. "It sounds perfect, but do you think she'll sing in front of anyone else?" His attention turned from trying to convince Jenny to one of his friends who had just arrived at the table, a camera hanging around his neck.

"What a big lens you have there," Brooke teased, licking her lips at him. The man laughed then ignored her comment.

"Ready?" he prompted Ethan.

As Ethan rose and walked towards the stage, Cam lent into Matthew. "A photographer. He's being ambitious, eh?"

Matthew chuckled and watched as Ethan got ready to play.

This should be fun, Cam thought to himself.

It was almost the end of the set and people stood and swayed all around them. For a one-man band in a little pub, Ethan got everyone moving and there wasn't an occupied seat that Cam could see.

Totally surprised at his natural presence on stage, Cam had to admit that Ethan's music wasn't hard to listen to, annoyingly. He stood with Jenny near their table. He clapped along but avoided actually dancing. The farm boy was doing well.

Matthew, Kelly and Brooke had made their way to the front when the music started and were using the little space they had to dance, shaking their bodies to the rhythm. After a song ended, Ethan paused, a middle-aged blonde woman shrieked with Ethan-mania.

"Though, I want to dedicate the next song to the person I love…" Ethan looked over at Jenny who was turning beetroot red, "I can't."

The crowd replied to him with a drawl of "ahhs."

Ethan continued, "Someone else in this room loves somebody very much and has a special question to ask…" Voices gabbled excitedly and someone produced a high-pitched whistle, adding to the tension.

Before Cam could take in Ethan's words, his heart quickened and his fists clenched. Ahead, Matthew got down on one knee, in front of his sister.

CHAPTER 12

At the kitchen island in Ethan's house, Jenny watched the scene unfolding outside of the window. Ethan's mother placed a mug of tea in front of her.

"They've been at it for an hour now," Alison said.

Her eyes moved to Ethan and Bryce who were out in the yard. Clouds of warm air trailed behind them with every exhale they made in the freezing, outside air. They were flipping tractor tyres.

"I bet they're sweating in those hats. Stupid reason for it, too. Though, I'm glad they are doing something together."

Jenny grinned. She could still picture Bryce's face when he knocked on Ethan's bedroom door, the night he decided he wanted to get muscles.

It couldn't have been easy for the seventeen-year-old to seek advice from his older brother. Bryce had lowered his head, looking at Ethan from underneath his long fringe, as he entered the room when he asked, "How do I get muscles?"

Feeling slightly guilty she was present, Jenny had hit Ethan in the stomach when he started to belly laugh.

"What do you want muscles for?", he chuckled. "Is Dad not working you hard enough on the farm?"

Giving Jenny a sidewards glance, Bryce admitted, "There's this girl in sixth form. She likes guys with muscles, alright? I need some."

He'd shuffled his feet and Ethan had raised an eyebrow at him. So, a week later, there they were, flipping tractor tyres to build him some muscles. Two bodies that would break an infrared camera in the Baltic temperature outside.

"Soo... Matthew and Kelly getting married?"

57

Alison's voice trailed off, probing for inside information from Jenny. Ethan's mother loved to gossip. Still trying to decipher how she felt about it, Jenny only nodded. It had been a week since the proposal and it was still the most popular topic of conversation, one she couldn't be a part of yet.

Jenny was happy for them. Kelly and Matthew balanced one another out perfectly. Seeing Cam's reaction that night, however, ruined her celebratory mood. The image of his eyes widening and perspiration forming on his forehead filled her mind. She knew Cam was hurting. Seeing his sister get proposed to must have stirred up a lot of mucky feelings for him, especially after being blindsided.

In his father's absence, Cam expected the person marrying Kelly to ask his permission first. Even as a kid, he would talk about how tough he would make it for them and they would laugh together.

Even though they were grown now, Jenny knew how important it was to him. Matthew hadn't told anyone of his plans, no indication, Ethan found out ten minutes before his set.

Why the hell didn't he talk to Cam first?

She recalled reaching for Cam's arm and giving it a reassuring squeeze. There was little she could do but be there for him if he needed her. He left before the others returned from the dance floor. He had Gemma, a girlfriend, to go to now, despite, all their lives, people expecting her and Cam to become a couple.

"A nice couple when you're older, you two," the neighbours would say. "Cam and Jenny sitting in a tree," the neighbourhood children would sing. The snarky comments from their peers in comprehensive school came later, but it all fell on deaf ears.

Unknown to the others, they had an unyielding friendship fuelled by Cam's desire for a stable family and Jenny's desire for a sibling. Cam moved into the house opposite just when Jenny was enduring her parent's grief. They were unable to bring her newly born brother home from the hospital. They still couldn't talk about it. In turn, Jenny and her still-together parents were there when Cam watched his father leave, days after they moved into the house.

It was through their heartache, an unbreakable bond formed, and it only carried on strengthening as they grew up together. It had been strange, Cam being so absent the last year, but Ethan had kept her occupied.

"Those boys." Ethan's dad entered the kitchen, breaking her thoughts. He shook his head and Jenny watched snow fall off his bobble hat onto the floor. "Flipping tractor tyres to build muscles? Ridiculous! I should have had them pull the rake at harvest, that would have done the trick."

He kissed Alison on the cheek,

"Hi, Jenny," he beamed.

"Let me move from your seat!" Jenny jumped from the stool and moved to the one alongside it. She knew it was Norman's favourite spot.

"Don't be soft, gal," he said but settled into the stool anyway.

Alison put the kettle on before starting to peel some potatoes.

"Want some help with those?" Jenny offered.

"That would be lovely. You wash and I'll peel?"

Happy to help, Jenny nodded and rolled up her sleeves, joining Alison who stood at the sink. Through the window, she could see that the yard was now empty and the tyres lay exhausted on the ground. Heavy footsteps emanated from the door and, a moment later, Ethan and Bryce appeared.

"Smelled the tea, did you?" their dad joked. "How are your muscles coming on, boy?" he felt Bryce's upper arms in jest as he passed. "Durr, almost as thick as those noodles you eat."

Bryce only huffed.

"How *humerus*, Dad," Ethan quipped.

"Leave the dad jokes to me, eh, Eth?"

Jenny laughed but her cheeks began to burn as Ethan wrapped his arms around her. She hated him making a display in front of his parents.

"Sure there's no tea for you?" his father directed at Ethan, who shook his head.

"No thanks, Dad." Ethan grabbed a cold drink from the fridge.

"My son – a *farmer* – doesn't like hot drinks. Even in this weather! Dew Dew."

Ethan and Jenny shared a glance. "Off for a quick shower" Ethan tapped Bryce on the shoulder as he departed, calling back,

"Good power hour bro."

"What on earth is a power hour?" Norman asked, making Jenny laugh out loud along with Alison. She loved this family.

CHAPTER 13

(Six Months Later)

The breeze was warm and the early morning sun was strong on Ethan's back. Stood with a nail in his mouth, he hammered another into a wooden post. Only five more metres of chicken wire fence to fix. Driving a final nail into the post, he heard his phone bleep. He dropped his hammer and pulled the phone out of his Levis. It was Jenny.

From Jenny:
Just leaving for work, can't wait to see you later
<3 xx.

Where he was standing, he could almost see her street on the opposite hillside. His eyes moved as if they were tracing her car moving up the steep hill. He could never actually see it because of the angle, but it didn't stop him looking. It had become his favourite view.

The sun was hitting both the hillsides now and he paused, taking in the sight. The songs came to him with no effort lately. Bright happy chords filled his mind while he worked and, when he picked up the guitar, the songs wrote themselves.

He thought back to his grandfather's hands moving up and down the neck of the guitar when he showed Ethan how to play. That was the best gift Ethan ever got: the gift of music.

Even if it was only locals in the pub enjoying his songs, it gave Ethan thrills each time he played to a crowd and it was all thanks to Jenny.

Before picking his hammer back up, he texted Jenny back a kiss and a love heart emoji.

Whistling a tune, he finished fixing the rest of the fence. He couldn't imagine not working on the farm but the thrill of having people sing, or even nod along to his music, was something he wanted to pursue.

***

Jenny loved an office day. It was nice to catch up with the others in her team. Driving down a hill that led to a nearby bypass, she took a couple of seconds to appreciate how beautiful the valley looked in the morning sun. Stopping at a red light, she looked up at Ethan's farm.

Where might he be right now? A warm sensation filled her as she remembered their tumble in the barn yesterday. If Bryce noticed the hay in their hair, he didn't say anything.

She wound down the window, letting fresh air flow through the car. Her new air freshener was too strong for the small space. Fed up with Jenny being home late because of cancelled trains and broken-down buses, her parents had bought her first little run-around and she loved it. It was old, but her bright red little beauty got her everywhere she needed to be.

Parking outside the business complex, she spotted Ashleigh heading towards the entrance. Bag in hand, she rushed out of the car, calling out for her to wait.

She had heard from Sam that Ashleigh was having a rough time in her assigned school. After telling her, he asked if Jenny knew where the school was. They were considering having her take over.

Ashleigh gave her a wave and stood in the doorway, holding the door open for her.

"Hi, Jen," her face was void of expression as Jenny grabbed the handle and followed her in.

"Thanks. Sorry I haven't texted much. You okay?"

Ashleigh shrugged. "I will be when we finish."

Using her fob to enter through more internal doors, Ashleigh didn't continue the conversation. Hesitant to pry, Jenny followed her in silence. They approached the last door that led to the office.

That's when Ashleigh asked, "How's Prince Charming? I can imagine that's why you haven't been texting."

Jenny brushed off Ashleigh's tone and replied, "He's doing great. Thinking about releasing his music soon."

"Good stuff," was all Ashleigh said before they entered the room, greeted by the smell of strong coffee and toast.

Relieved to be around cheerful people again Jenny headed for her usual hot desk. She had ten pupil reports to write up and didn't want to fall behind with the school holidays approaching.

Ten minutes later the room was quiet. Only clacking keyboard keys and the occasional shuffling of papers broke the silence. The double doors of the office entrance opened and her manager, Sam, and the company's director walked in.

"Sorry to disturb you all. I know it is your admin day and you have lots to do," Sam declared before Pearl, the company's director took over.

"We would be grateful if you could give us a few moments of your time and meet us in the upstairs training room, 1:00 pm." The group shared quizzical glances when they both left the room.

"I can't stand her," Ashleigh announced when she was sure they had gone.

"Did she manage to get you a new placement, Ash?" asked Brie, filling the silence Ashleigh's statement left.

"No, no she did not. I'm staying there."

After lunch, Jenny tried to keep happy thoughts in the forefront of her mind, Ethan's texts helped her do that:

From Ethan:
Bryce is covering the shift on
the farm tomorrow. It's my first gig in
Cardiff and we can stay at yours afterwards! <3
I'm one lucky man ;) xxxx

She entered the training room behind Brie and Ashleigh. The small group that trained together remained and they still fitted along the front desk, facing the white board. Pearl entered next. For a small woman, she held an air of authority that made Jenny's hair stand on end.

"Thank you all for being here, and so promptly." She paused to check everyone was listening. "Sam sends his apologies. There is an urgent matter he needs to attend to. Firstly, I want to thank you all for being here and working hard, helping us grow the business and for helping hundreds of children reach their full potential." Pearl's body was rigid as she spoke, only her eyes moved making the speech eerie.

"I was unable to meet you during your training but, from the reports I have been receiving, it's clear we have an excellent team and I'm grateful for your dedication."

John clapped and her hardened face softened in surprise.

"My speech isn't over, unfortunately," added Pearl. John held up his palm in apology and the team tried to hold back their giggles. "We like to award our staff and give credit where it's due. Hence, I'm pleased to confirm that Sam has put forward two of your names to undertake additional duties and, of course, that comes with extra compensation." The room went silent. "I will speak to those who have been put forward and hope that, as a team, you see this as a collective opportunity rather than a loss for those not selected."

Pearl's eyes brushed over them one by one, gauging their reactions. At the same time, Jenny caught glances from the others, already sizing one another up, wondering who was put forward. Wiggling in her seat to help her feel a little more comfortable, she looked again to Pearl who had not yet finished.

"We like to celebrate our wins and have planned a company conference – an all-inclusive evening that we will run annually. There will be awards, food, beverages and entertainment. Sam will send an email with the information. This is a mandatory event for staff. We would not be a company without you."

Speech finished, Pearl headed for the door. Before opening it, though, she stated, "I'll be in my office for the rest of today if anyone has questions. You may now resume your work downstairs."

She opened the door and watched them leave in silence, one by one.

"Pretty tense in there," John exhaled in the corridor, Jenny nodded. "What do you think of it, Jen?"

He seemed excited, but Jenny shrugged, really hoping it was her bound for the promotion.

"Well, I'm not one for wanting more work but I sure as heck wouldn't decline the pay rise," John continued.

He held the door open for those behind him.

"Amen to that!" Brie replied.

John raised his hand and they high-fived. Jenny and Ashleigh remained silent as they returned to their desks opposite each other.

With an hour left of the day, Pearl had called John to her office. When he left, the tension in the room rose significantly. Sneaking a glance at her phone, Jenny started reading a text from Ethan when Sam entered the room.

"Jen, can we borrow you please?"

John hadn't returned yet. Jenny got up and discreetly slipped her phone into her bag before following him out of the room. Did this mean she was being offered more duties? She flexed her fingers and bit her lip. Not knowing how to feel, she followed Sam, staring down at the blue carpet until they reached the office.

***

"That's amazing. Well done!" was Ethan's first reaction. Glad to be away from the office and the disappointed faces of her colleagues, Jenny wished the promotion felt like a win rather than a betrayal.

They sat in the top field of the hillside in the back of the farm's pickup truck, watching the traffic of commuters returning to their homes in the valley below.

She let out a sigh and Ethan pulled her into him. Laying against his chest, she relaxed, listening to the steady sound of his heartbeat.

"Sorry about the sweat," he laughed. She didn't move, she just stayed there. The breeze in the top field drew goosebumps on her arms.

Jenny was gratified to be selected but when she learnt those duties included supervising Ashleigh in her assigned school, it filled her with dread. A supervisor to her colleagues. *Was she up for that?*

"Should we make a move?" Ethan asked, noticing the goosebumps. "Mam's making stew."

Jenny hopped off the back of the truck. "Yeah, we can go. I could stare at this view all day though. I love being up here."

Ethan nodded in agreement, his eyes not leaving her. "It would be a better view if I knew that's where you used to live…" His voice trailed off as he looked in the direction of her street.

"Used to live?" she repeated and stared at him with a raised eyebrow.

Ethan couldn't contain his excitement. Jumping down from the back of the truck, he grabbed her hand.

"My parents are willing to sell us the guest house. I want to live with you. Move in with me, Jen?"

Jenny paused, trying to hide the shock from her face as she took in what he asked. She knew she had a bad poker face because he hesitated. Her hand was warm as it squeezed his. She turned away from him and refused to look back. Not knowing how to react, she acted like she wasn't paying attention.

"Let's go get some of that stew," she said, dropping his hand and heading for the passenger side of the truck.

All the while, she could almost hear Ethan's thoughts: *That didn't go to plan.*

CHAPTER 14

The high street was bustling as usual on a Saturday. By night, kebab shops opened and takeaways thrived, the street was littered with teenagers and drunks. It was something you wouldn't believe looking at it in the daytime. Salons, chic boutiques and cute coffee shops brightened it, presenting the illusion of sophistication and class to those not familiar with the area.

Bella's was their favourite cafe. The owner was always enthusiastic as she greeted them. Her pink lipstick matched the floral wallpaper that covered the walls. The sound of the coffee machine foaming milk and blenders whizzing added to the excitable vibrations of chatter that emanated from people sat at the polka-dot-dressed tables.

Tucked away in their usual corner, Kelly eagerly waited for their lattes to be delivered to the table. Her eyes kept darting to her bag containing her design book and the beautiful dresses they would wear for the biggest day of her life.

"So, about this engagement party…" Jenny trailed off. "How come you've decided to do one now, six months after the proposal?"

Smiling at the waitress who carried the rich smelling coffee towards them, Kelly replied. "Better late than never. The dresses I've designed for the wedding may take a while to make. I'm hoping the party will help keep our engagement relevant."

Jenny nodded. Brooke, meanwhile, was staring into her phone, missing their conversation. Jenny tapped Brooke's leg with her foot. Nodding at an absent question, Brooke lowered her phone to the table.

"Someone interesting?" Kelly asked.

Jenny scanned her face for clues. Used to Brooke spieling off a description of a man from a dating app, they were surprised to see her expression change to a Bambi-like one. Her eyes widened and you could see her trying to choose her words.

"Brooke…" Jenny nudged. "Spill the beans."

"Umm, no one. It's all good!" She picked up the tall glass and sipped her latte. "That's so good… what were we talking about?"

Letting Brooke change the conversation, Kelly placed the large binder in the centre of the table. Opening the hard front cover, she revealed her first sketches. Two dresses with a colour code of midnight blue in the bottom right-hand corner. They were designed to complement figures that mirrored Jenny and Brooke's body shapes.

Brooke's mouth hung open. "These are beautiful, Kel! Not very bridal but stunning. You're planning on making these? Which one and why blue?"

Kelly rolled her eyes and Jenny's mouth raised at the corner.

"They're for you, Silly! Look, here's yours. It'll compliment your tiny waist with the stitching here. And here's your dress, Jen. It hugs in all the right places to enhance your shape."

"These are fabulous, Kel. You and your mam are going to make a killing making dresses like these."

"I do have to ask, though…" added Brooke, "Why are you making dresses for us?."

There was another silent pause. Jenny and Kelly looked at Brooke whose eyes flitted between them until the penny dropped.

"No! Are you serious? We get to be bridesmaids?" Brooke's face lit up and her hand cupped her mouth.

"Taa Daa." Kelly did jazz hands, making them all giggle.

Jenny didn't think Kelly would want her standing next to her on her big day. Her relationship with Cam always seemed to be a barrier between them in their friendship. This was good news, though.

Jenny leaned forward, peering at Kelly's book. "I don't know what to say, but definitely yes!" Her face reflected the glow Kelly emanated.

"It's a yes from me, too! I hope we get to see what you have in mind for *your* dress!"

Animated by their reactions, Kelly turned the page. Brooke's phone illuminated on the table as she did it, though. An unwelcome distraction. The sudden noise and vibration caused Kelly to drop the page she was lifting.

Jenny peered over to Brooke's phone curious to see the caller ID. But before she could read a name, Brooke slapped her hand over the screen, covering it from view.

"Everything okay, Brooke?" Jenny asked, not wanting to add to the tension that sizzled from Brooke.

The phone stopped ringing but, after only a few seconds, it rang again. Brooke growled out loud as she hit the reject button.

"Look I'm sorry, okay." She didn't look at either of them but tried to compose herself. Jenny shot a quick look at Kelly whose eyes had widened.

"I've been a bad friend to you, Jen. I feel awful."

Jenny leaned back with her eyebrows raised, watching Brooke who had slumped next to her. She shot a nervous glance at Kelly who was leaning in closer waiting for Brooke's explanation. They were used to her theatrics but she was never this dramatic.

"What for?" Jenny asked.

After a deep breath and exhale, Brooke finally relieved her conscience. "I've been seeing Dan, your ex. I'm sorry, we've become 'a thing.'" Brooke bit her lip. In an attempt to stifle a chuckle, Jenny snorted, causing a contagious laugh to break out between her and Kelly. Trying to regain composure after noting Brooke's nervous expression, Jenny wiped a tear of laughter and straightened her face.

"How the heck did that happen?" Kelly asked.

"I bumped into him. I know he should be off-limit being your ex, but we just get on really well and…"

Brooke watched Jenny's amused expression

"Let me guess, you can't stop him from calling you now?" Jenny said with a grin, knowing how needy Dan could be.

Brooke shook her head. Her curly hair bounced with the movement. "It sounds stupid but that's what I like about him. It's nice to be wanted, even if it's all the time. You two are all loved up. Now I am, too."

Jenny placed her hand on Brooke's.

"If you're happy then I am. He's a good guy. You suit."

"There is one thing I must request, though."

Jenny felt Brooke's body stiffen next to her.

"What?" She stared at Jenny as if wondering what she might have to do to maintain her relationship and their friendship.

"Text him and tell him you'll call him back after your coffee? Kelly might burst if we don't go back to planning." Brooke blushed and Kelly grinned, "Good Idea."

Pulling into her parents' driveway was always a relief. Jenny remembered the time she climbed out the bathroom window onto the side porch roof to sneak out with Cam, only for her dad to be surprised as he stepped out of the door to put out the bins. At the time, she had landed on the grass in front of him.

It felt good to have a moment to think about all the memories. There were no signs of wear or tear on the house. It was a warm and loved home that never changed.

Could I really move from the street? she wondered.

She rummaged in her bag for her house key. It was starting to look worn, covered in black paw prints which reminded her of Kiki, their Labrador.

Before leaving the car, Jenny looked to the living room window and, sure enough, Kiki was there, paws resting on the windowsill, her mouth open wide in greeting, willing Jenny to come inside. Jenny could picture her tail thrashing as she approached the house. She felt a warm feeling in her gut. This was home. Did she feel like this at Ethan's house? Could she move?

After Brooke disclosed she was seeing Dan, Jenny didn't want to interrupt Kelly's planning further by telling them Ethan wanted her to move in with him. It was a decision she needed to make on her own.

CHAPTER 15

Mucking out a stall was the least glamorous job of owning a horse. Luckily, the worming was left to the vet. The livery on the farm was stocked with the horses of other owners but one stall was kept for Bluey, Ethan's horse. Ethan stood, thinking of the bond that Jenny had developed with Bluey. That horse loved Jenny as much as Ethan did. The grey palomino was out enjoying himself grazing with the other colts in the field, leaving Ethan to clean up his mess.

Like I don't have enough on, Ethan thought to himself, remembering it was his turn to clean the cow pen, too.

He was almost done with his last pile to shovel when he heard footsteps crunching on the gravel, towards the stable. Dropping the rake, he took off his gloves and leant against one of the stall beams, smiling as he watched Jenny enter. When she got closer, he swooped in an lifted her off the ground, her bum cheeks resting on his strong arms. There, he held her, looking up as she giggled. She lowered her head and he spun, locking lips with her as he lowered her to the ground.

"Well hello," she said as they broke apart. "Just saw Bluey in the field. He's having a whale of a time rolling around."

"Lucky him. I wish we were rolling around." Ethan leant in and kissed her again. This time, he was the one that pulled away. "Got good news for me? Have you decided yet?" Watching her expression change, he guessed the answer. "You don't want to move in together?"

He couldn't control the hardened expression in his face and returned to finish the last bit of shovelling in the stall to hide it. As he shovelled the last pile, she tutted. He knew she was rolling her eyes behind him. After a couple of seconds, he stopped and turned to look at her, resting his hands on the handle of the shovel, waiting for her to have her say.

"We spend most nights together. Neither of us have any real savings. I'm just getting used to my new role at work." She took a deep breath, shuffling the hay on the ground with her feet, then continued. "I'm not sure I'm ready to leave my parents in all honesty. It sounds stupid but I'm not."

She said it with clarity and he felt his facial muscles soften, his body following suit. He didn't want to push her into doing something she didn't want. He and his family loved having her here. It was hard to accept it didn't feel like home to her yet.

The corners of his mouth rose.

"I'm sorry," he stated, leaning the shovel against the side of the stall. Walking to her again, he wrapped his thick arms around her, holding her tightly to show he meant it.

"No, I'm sorry," she said weakly. "It would be great to live here, just not right now." He said nothing but lowered his head and teased her lips with his. When they paused, she looked at him with a mischievous twinkle in her eye. "Still happy to have me stay the night, though?"

Ethan snorted before locking eyes with her.

"Always"

Ethan's eyes opened like clockwork. Used to rushing to put on his clothes to begin the animal feeds and other gruelling tasks on the farm, he took a moment. Looking at Jenny's shape curled up underneath the quilt beside him, he felt a deep feeling of adoration. The quilt was tucked under her chin. Releasing a breath, he let the feelings of doubt and disappointment that plagued him through the night subside.

The irrationality of rejection poked holes in his thoughts but he knew they had time and he didn't need to rush her. She was with him. That's all that mattered.

Quietly he got out of bed and slid on his clothes. Trying not to disturb her, he opened the door. Then, changing his mind, he tiptoed back to the bed and planted a kiss on her forehead, watching the corner of her mouth rise as she dreamed.

You'll change your mind, he thought as he departed.

Already, he was eager to get his jobs finished and get back to her. Maybe even before breakfast started.

His dad greeted him with a grin. Stood at the fridge, he took out a bottle of milk and an orange juice carton for Ethan.

"No tea?" Norman chuckled. Every morning he asked this question, as if it were the most bizarre thing that a farmer's boy preferred cold beverages over a cup of tea. "You never know; you might change your mind one day."

Ethan only rolled his eyes in response.

"At least we don't have to bother prepping forage for the cows yet." Norman tapped Ethan's back like he usually did when Ethan needed a reminder they had to get on with the work, however tiring. "Drink up."

CHAPTER 16

(Four Months Later)

Cam's and Jack's black polished shoes clattered over the marble flooring as they approached the hotel front desk. They watched as a well-groomed lady rose in greeting.

"CJ and Co.?" she queried, a broad grin frozen on her face.

Jack nodded in response. Returning to her seat, the receptionist picked up a telephone and spoke, alerting the person on the other end of their arrival.

"Mr Plunkett's assistant will be down to collect you momentarily." Smiling politely, she added, "Please take a seat in our waiting area." Her eyes flitted to a set of small, bright orange stools placed around a quirky green table. They were in the middle of a large, open space in front of an elevator. These stools were far too small for either of them to sit.

Rolling his eyes, Cam followed Jack, heading to loiter around the bizarre furniture until Mr Plunkett's assistant arrived. He loved sharing the new enterprise with Jack. Some of their customers, on the other hand, he did not. Unfortunately, they didn't have the luxury of being picky, yet.

"Ready for this pitch?" Jack asked and Cam grinned back, knowing Jack already knew the answer.

Mr Plunkett, with his prized chain of spas and hotels, had dominated the press lately. A cocktail of scandalous claims of adultery combined with whistleblowing employees and alleged emotional abuse towards his wife had all increased the media speculation.

Being subjective, Cam didn't like the man. Getting to work with a chain worth millions of pounds, however, was not an opportunity a newly established PR and Marketing company could reject easily.

The ping of the elevator sounded, followed by opening doors that revealed Mr Plunkett's assistant. High-heeled strides echoed on the reception's marble floor and Cam looked to see Jack's jaw drop in awe.

"Hi, I'm Becky." The assistant held out her hand to Jack first. His dazzling smile was in full action.

"I'm Jack," he said. "And this is –"

"– You must be Cam." She exclaimed before he could finish.

In turn, Becky held her hand out to Cam. He noted her surprisingly firm grip.

"Nice to meet you, CJ & Co.," she said through smiling white teeth. Her bright red lips and cherry-coloured heels contrasted with the black slim-fit suit she wore. "Please, follow me."

Acknowledging them both once more, she turned and walked towards the waiting elevator. Her long ponytail swished against her back as she walked. Raising their eyebrows at one another, they followed dutifully, briefcases held at their sides.

They were both smiling as they exited the hotel.

"I think it went well," Cam said in the fresh air.

"So do I," Jack agreed.

"And you got a date with that Becky bird, eh? Not a total waste of time if we don't get the contract."

Jack scoffed as if he knew that wasn't a possibility.

"How come you accepted her invitation?" Cam asked.

Jack had sworn off dates and women, though there were plenty of opportunities.

"She asked me to a gig. She might be different."

Cam nodded in understanding.

"Well let me know how it goes, Jacky-boy."

Jack rolled his eyes.

"See you Monday."

Both looking pleased, they went their separate ways.

CHAPTER 17

Jenny watched blurs of brightly coloured winter coats flash past the frosted window. Ice crystals on the glass prevented her from seeing the children who were likely laughing as they played outside in a yard dusted with snow.

Ashleigh entered the room holding two cups of coffee.

"It's not the hard stuff but gosh we need to celebrate!"

The corners of Jenny's mouth rose and she gratefully accepted the steaming hot cup.

Helping Ashleigh retain St. Bernard's School as a customer had to be the biggest highlight of Jenny's career so far. With the school being in a disadvantaged area, a tight budget and even tighter timeframe for improvements, it was a momentous task trying to raise attainment levels.

Using lots of intervention strategies, though, they had succeeded and not only proved the worth of their work but the worth of the school, improving the lives of the children who attended it. When they were told the school avoided being placed under special measures that morning, Jenny and Ashleigh burst into a mini-dance.

"Thanks for your help, Jen. It really means a lot. I'm glad you were assigned to me after the promotion."

Jenny frowned. She still didn't like the way it sounded. The reality of having to instruct a peer wasn't fun, but she and Ashleigh had made it work.

"I hardly did anything," she said modestly. "Anyway, you have any plans this weekend?"

Jenny blew on the coffee and hoped it would cool in time for her to drink before the children came back inside.

"No, my friends don't go out often. Probably just a weekend watching Netflix." There was sadness in her voice. "How about you, Jen? Ethan got any gigs on?"

Jenny took a sip of the coffee but it burned her tongue. *Still too hot.*

"He does, actually. It's in the city, too. You should come," Jenny offered with excitement. It would be nice to have company watching Ethan play.

"Oh," said Ashleigh, surprised at the offer. "I could finally meet Prince Charming."

"Yep, and we can celebrate with something stronger than coffee." Jenny winked.

"Amen to that!"

A handheld bell ringing in the school yard followed Ashleigh's excitement, and Jenny sighed.

Time to get back to work.

CHAPTER 18

Jenny drove on autopilot to Cam's and Gemma's house. Her visits were becoming frequent now she worked in schools in the city. Stopping off there helped her stay in touch with them and shake the stress of the day off before returning home.

A car beeped, the driver wanting her to go when the traffic light turned amber. She hated city traffic but envied the lack of commute Gemma and Cam had to their little cul-de-sac. It only took a few moments to reach. Tapping the front door gently to make them aware of her arrival, she let herself in without waiting.

The hallway was small and faced the stairs. Jenny slipped off her shoes and entered the door to the left that led to the living room. Gemma greeted her from where she stood ironing her nurse's uniform in front of the TV.

"Hello, hope you don't mind me popping in?" Jenny asked. The house always smelled like a Yankee Candle shop.

"Hi, Jen!" Gemma replied brightly. She placed the iron upright on the board and moved around it to embrace her.

"Course not. You're always welcome!"

They could hear Cam talking in the kitchen and Jenny raised an eyebrow. Gemma shrugged.

"Work stuff, I think. He's on the phone with Jack again."

Jenny still hadn't met Cam's business partner Jack. She hadn't heard much about him, either, considering Cam spent most of his days with him. He never spoke about him.

"Make yourself comfy. Cuppa?" Gemma opened the door to the kitchen and Cam's voice sounded louder. A moment later, she returned holding a cup of tea and Cam was just behind her holding two. They were an ideal couple.

If I didn't get wasted that night, they might have never met, she thought.

"Hey, Jen. How was work?"

"Pretty good today, actually. How's it going with the business?"

Cam's smile widened so much there wasn't much room left for his cheeks. "Really good. We just landed Plunkett Enterprises as a client." He did a fist pump in the air.

"Like, Plunket Enterprises who own all those hotels?" Jenny's eyes widened in surprise.

"That's the one!"

"Congratulations, babe." Gemma placed tea down next to Jenny. "You and Jack are unstoppable."

"We're quite the dream team," Cam said coyly.

"Yeah, congratulations! That's honestly the best news!" Jenny added. Cam beamed and sipped his tea.

"Does this mean we may not need a lodger?" Gemma asked with a nervous laugh.

"Lodger?!" Jenny asked.

"Yeah," Cam grimaced. "Bills have been higher than usual and the landlord's upping the rent. We've been considering it."

"Fair," Jenny nodded. Everyone was finding the cost of living tough. Living with her parents and being back and forth Ethan's house, she had it easy. "Still, I'm sure it'll sort itself out. You're both working hard. You'll reap the rewards, I'm sure!"

"Thanks, Jen," said Cam

"So will you," added Gemma. "Any plans for you and Ethan on the horizon?"

Jenny shrugged but saw Cam look at her suspiciously. He always knew when she was withholding information.

"Ethan asked me to move in with him a few months back, but I'm just not ready to leave Mam and Dad's still. Is that awful?" she asked, beginning to doubt herself.

"Course not," Gemma reassured her. "You'll know when the time's right! You both seem perfect together, but – take it from us – save your pennies. It's not cheap!"

Jenny took a sip of the tea that had rapidly cooled.

"Are you sure you can't come to Ethan's gig tomorrow night?"

"Sorry, beaut. I'm working"

"Me, too. Sorry, Jen. No rest with the plans me and Jack have," seconded Cam.

"Well, okay…" Jenny trailed off.

Sensing her disappointment, Gemma added, "Don't forget, you're welcome here anytime. We have the spare bedroom. If it saves you and Ethan on taxis, or you ever need to crash, it's not a problem."

Jenny grinned and thanked her, then finished the last of her tea.

"Are you going to yours tonight, Jen, or Ethan's?" Cam asked when she indicated she was about to leave.

"Ethan's."

Cam retrieved a very long pair of black suit trousers from Gemma's ironing pile.

"If it's not too much trouble, could you drop these in the shop for me? Need them altered. Kelly said she's in the shop late or you can drop them to Mam's.

"Sure, I need to see Kelly about the engagement party anyway. I'll swing by the high street before Ethan's." Jenny rose and pulled her bag to her shoulder. Taking the trousers off Cam, she draped them over her arm. Even then, they almost touched the floor.

"Thanks, both. See you soon."

They followed her to the door to wave her off.

"Only move in with Ethan when you're ready, Jen!" Cam called before she got in the car.

"Drive safe," Gemma added. Jenny nodded at them both.

They'll make great parents one day.

CHAPTER 19

It was 6:00 pm when Jenny reached the high street. As per usual for Friday nights, girls in long dresses and thick fur coats walked towards the train station, presumably heading to the city. A group of men, all wearing shirts, headed towards the closest pubs situated around a corner. As a group, they eyed up the women as they passed.

Most of the shops had closed, leaving the businesses of the night open. At least she had a good chance at parking in the temporary bays this late.

Pulling outside *The Little Valley Designer,* Kelly's shop, Jenny looked at the light that glowed from beneath a lowered shutter onto the pavement. Kelly was still there.

Jenny didn't blame Kelly for lowering the shutter in the dark, for both privacy and security. The high street could be an eerie place when you're alone.

Thinking about how creepy the silent street could be, she tapped on the shutters gently, not wanting to scare Kelly. There, she waited, hands tucked into her high waisted coat pockets. She glanced down to make sure Cam's trousers remained draped over her arm. A motor noise sounded, followed by the shutters clattering as they began to rise. They stopped at the halfway point.

"Sorry, Jen, can you duck under?" Kelly's head appeared under the shutters, "They get stuck if I open them fully from the inside. Stupid things."

Jenny ducked under the shutter as instructed, awkwardly squatting to enter. She hadn't been in the shop since Kelly's and Cam's mother first opened it. Kelly had graduated with a BA honours in Fashion and Design. The shop was bare back then compared to how it looked today.

To Jenny's left was a display of shabby chic gifts, to her right, a till area, decorated with framed pictures of bright floral dress sketches. Jenny stroked a cream, knitted blanket on display and thought it replicated how the shop felt: warm and cosy.

Ahead of her was a glass room that afforded customers a view of the working area. A large whiteboard took up most of the wall. Beautiful handwriting detailed jobs of the day, collection dates and times. In the centre of the room was a Singer sewing machine. To the left of the till, a corridor led to a glass room in which two clothes racks stood full of hanging garments, carefully covered in polythene bags and neatly hung with the receipts clipped to them, ready to collect

"Don't look," Kelly instructed her. She rubbed her brow and turned away from the racks that looked fit to burst. "People are a nightmare; eager to give me their clothes but they never want to collect them!" She complained before asking curiously. "Aren't you meant to be at Ethan's? Tracey picked Mam up and said you were at his tonight."

"Ahh, yeah, I forgot it was wine night," said Jenny. "I'm heading to Ethan's after dropping off these. While I'm here, by the way, can I get your list of supplies for the engagement party? It's not long now."

Kelly laughed "You're too organised, I need to hire you, I think!"

Jenny stopped looking at the trinkets that caught her eye and she faced Kelly, taking in the pale hair that was wrapped in a messy bun on the top of her head. Her eyes looked dark underneath.

"What time have you been here since, Kel?"

"5:00 am." Kelly admitted. "The orders and alterations have been crazy busy. Not that that's a bad thing."

Jenny watched Kelly's scan a stack of clothes piled on a countertop next to the till. The calendar next to the pile had lots of thin red sticky notes dotted all over it. There was no doubt in her mind; Kelly needed help.

"Got a kettle here?" she asked finally. "I'll make you a cuppa."

"Thank you," Kelly said, looking relieved. "It's in the back."

Being careful not to disturb the already high pile, Jenny

added Cam's trousers to the top, removing her hands slowly so the pile didn't topple.

"I won't be a moment," she said.

Kelly frowned, playing with the receipt paper in the till. "I hope Cam knows he won't be getting these anytime soon. Don't they have seamstresses in Cardiff?"

Jenny didn't respond. She knew Kelly would be offended if Cam went to anyone else.

Stopping after the glass room, she peered through a door into what looked like a dressing room with a smart, grey chair, a full-sized mirror and a naked mannequin. Passing it, she entered a second, tiny room with just a makeshift counter holding a microwave, kettle and toaster. She flipped a switch and, as the kettle started to boil, she heard Kelly coo, approaching the room.

"While you're here, Jen, got time for me to take measurements for your bridesmaid dress?"

Jenny was tempted to check the time before answering but she felt the weight of Kelly's excitable gaze.

"Of course," she grinned, wondering if Ethan had tried to call her yet. She was already late.

"Remind me why you want to make the dresses from scratch when you're this busy?" she asked playfully.

"Honestly, I think I just miss garment construction. It was my favourite part of my degree. It's nice to make clothes that fit people without them needing altering." A spark ignited in Kelly's eyes as she spoke.

The kettle switched off.

"Go on, I'll make us the cuppa. I know where everything is," said Kelly, squeezing past her and pulling out a box from underneath the counter containing pots of tea, coffee, sugar and hot chocolates.

"Okay, I just need to call Ethan quickly. Mind if I slip outside, Kel?"

"Not at all. Tell him I said Hi!" Kelly busied herself making tea as Jenny walked back to the front of the shop.

The high street was surprisingly quiet and the air was desperately cold compared to Kelly's warm shop. Dialling Ethan, Jenny hopped from one foot to the other in an attempt to move and keep herself warm.

"Hey, sorry I'm late. And I might be even later..." she started before Ethan could speak.

"No worries. You okay? Just about to lock up the animals with Bryce. What time will you get here?"

"Ah, well, I've dropped Cam's trousers off to Kelly and she's asked if she can take some measurements for the bridesmaid dress. Hopefully, it won't take too long. Should I get us some food on my way back?"

"Cam's trousers?" Ethan asked, puzzled.

"Yeah, he needed them taken up. I popped in to see him and Gemma. They're thinking of renting out their spare room." Her voice quivered as the cold seeped through her skin.

"Isn't one girl enough for him?" Ethan snapped down the phone.

"What?" Jenny's eyebrows furrowed. "What do you mean?"

"Is it not enough he's with Gemma? He wants you to move in, too? I hope you gave him the same reaction you gave me."

Jenny took a deep breath. She couldn't believe what she was hearing.

"Don't be ridiculous, I'm not moving anywhere, and Cam certainly doesn't have, or want, more than one girl!"

"Oh, come off it, Jen. Stop being so naive. He's only with Gemma because he can't have you."

Jenny was full on shivering now. She was freezing but adrenaline was starting to flow through her.

How dare you, she thought. If she and Cam liked each other in that way, they could have got together a long time ago. Ethan, of all people, should know them better. Know her better.

Keeping her voice steady and calm, she tried to recover this bizarre conversation.

"What makes you think that, Eth? Me and Cam have been best friends forever. Nothing's changed."

Ethan laughed.

"We were good friends too, Jen. We got together, didn't we? He's just biding his time like I did."

Jenny almost growled. "You're making no bloody sense, Eth! What the hell is wrong with you? You know what, I'm not coming over tonight. We need to cool off."

84

Silence ensued and the temperature outside seemed to drop even further.

"Are you still coming to my gig tomorrow?" Ethan asked, sounding defeated.

Jenny's brain rattled, trying to comprehend the emotions she felt.

What have I done to make him doubt me? Where did this conversation stem from?

"Probably," was all she said in response.

"Sorry, Jen," Ethan said before she hung up. He sounded deflated and but she didn't care. At that moment, all she wanted to do was attack him for the insult. He was lucky she restrained herself at all.

She entered the shop hoping Kelly had made the tea.

***

Throwing his phone onto the bed, Ethan couldn't believe the conversation he had just had with Jenny. Holding his palms to his temples, he knew their first real argument wouldn't be pretty but he wasn't prepared for how out-of-check his emotions had gotten.

Bryce calling him from downstairs interrupted his thoughts. He would have to process the conversation later. His brother had become more reliable than him. He let out an exhausted sigh.

"Come on, Eth. Cows ain't gonna feed themselves. They'll freeze without the extra grub."

Ethan followed Bryce's voice down to the kitchen, towards the back door where his wellies stood waiting for him.

The cold air from the back door hit him as he entered. Bryce stood outside, waiting for him in anticipation, mist forming with each breath he took.

"Sorry," Ethan managed as he pulled the heavy Hunters onto his feet.

"You know what Dad says. We let the boys starve, we starve."

Ethan was amused. Bryce sounded exactly like their dad when he had said it. He pictured his parents on their holiday. It was the worst time to be away with the cattle needing extra feeds and all the extra jobs that came along with winter. Norman's saying was true; if the Welsh Blacks lost weight, technically, so would they. He hoped they were having a good time, though, despite his inner grumble. It was their anniversary after all.

The air outside was still. Trudging up the slope towards the barn, he followed his brother's boot prints. Looking up, he saw his figure waiting for him in the distance: Bluey. The horse had his head over the fence, his turnout rug keeping the worst of the frost off him.

Ethan walked over and looked into his black eyes. As he stroked his muzzle, Ethan took a deep breath and felt himself become calmer. The horse nudged his hand away, demanding his usual sugar cube.

From his pocket Ethan pulled what Bluey was waiting for, two glistening cubes. Flattening his palm, he felt the warmth of the horse's mouth as he took the treats.

"Eth!" His brother shouted, causing Bluey's ears to prick. The horse turned his head curiously as he chewed the cubes.

Continuing up the hill, Bryce disappeared into the barn, but at least Bluey walked alongside him for company. He would make up for his slack with Bryce tonight. When they got home, he'd order them pizza and they could have a few beers. Jenny wasn't coming over now after all.

The air didn't feel much warmer inside the barn than the air outside. Bryce was right; it would be a freezer tonight. Luckily, Bryce had already stacked the alfalfa hay and was scooping the protein pellets into buckets. So, they shouldn't have to endure the cold for too long. Grabbing a bucket himself, Ethan filled it at twice the speed of Bryce, who had a head start.

"Who's pissed you off?" Bryce asked mockingly. Ethan pulled out his phone that was bleeping. It was a text from Rob, the promoter for his upcoming gig.

From Rob:
Got those two spare tickets you asked for. You're lucky.
It's sold out! See you tomorrow man.

He had done as Jenny had asked and got her and her friend from work tickets. Glad the gig was a sellout, Ethan hoped Jenny would show up to see it. Annoyed at how insecure he was feeling, he filled the next five buckets and began to haul them to the cowshed. Just Bluey left to lock in and he could figure out his next move.

CHAPTER 20

With the amount of time she spent in the city recently, Jenny thought she would have got used to the smell of exhaust fumes. She and Ashleigh stood waiting to cross the busy road outside the city centre train station. The air was thick and muggy.

Having Ashleigh for company and conversation helped to distract her from thinking about her argument with Ethan on the phone last night. As she thought about it, his harsh tone, a tone she had never heard him use. She let out an involuntary sigh.

"You okay, Jen? You don't seem yourself."

"Me and Ethan had our first argument last night. It wasn't good."

"I don't think any arguments are good, are they?" Ashleigh seemed pleased with her retort.

"I suppose not."

They both continued to walk, trying to avoid their heels slipping into the grooves of the tiled pavement. A low riding Renault drove towards them, appearing to slow as it did.

"Oi oi, love! Let's have your number then?" A boy younger than them stuck his head out of the window and looked directly at Ashleigh. The purple Fiat behind him blared the horn. Jenny watched as he strained to look back at them for a response but the driver had been forced to speed up.

"Bellend," Ashleigh muttered. Looking downwards, she crossed her arms over her chest.

Jenny let out an exaggerated sigh in sympathy. It seemed being beautiful did have its drawbacks. Ashleigh always looked effortlessly glamorous, even on a Monday morning. Without fail, her eyebrows were painted, lipstick framed her big smile and her warm honey-coloured hair always looked soft.

"Some people are just idiots," Jenny declared.

"You got that right! So, what's Prince Charming done to make you argue?"

They stopped at another set of traffic lights and waited for the stickman to turn green.

"I'm not really sure whose fault it is," Jenny admitted. "I think he got the wrong idea when I was telling him about my day. I mentioned Cam and Gemma were thinking about renting a room."

Ashleigh winced. "He thought you wanted to move in with them instead of with him?"

Jenny nodded but she couldn't hide the surprise on her face. Why would Ashleigh jump to the same conclusion? Jenny had not for one second considered moving in with them.

"Even good men can be idiots, Jen," Ashleigh retorted.

The night before she recalled complaining about her commute into the city, in hindsight, Jenny shouldn't have mentioned Cam might be renting a room. She and Ashleigh crossed the road.

"Did you make up?" Ashleigh asked, bringing her back from re-running the argument through her mind.

"I think so," said Jenny, though she wasn't really sure.

"Good," Ashleigh stated. "Even a fairytale couple need to have a conflict. It's the rule."

Jenny hoped that was all that it was. A conflict that would resolve itself.

CHAPTER 21

Jenny's mood had lifted by the time they finally approached the venue. Their heels unenthusiastically clattered beneath them as they both vowed to never trust walking time estimates on Google Maps ever again.

Though neither grand nor prestigious-looking from the outside, The Train Shack was hailed as one of the best live music spots to attend and play in Cardiff. It held enough people to make gigs feel like a real party but it was small enough that you were never too far away from the stage.

In his only text to her that day, Ethan sounded excited.

From Ethan:
Acoustics are great here Jen!
soundchecking now x

She'd responded with a smiley emoji paired with a guitar and heart icon. How were you meant to have a normal conversation after an argument?

There was a courtyard of sorts outside the building. Inside were two enormous doors supported by a singular thick beam in the centre. It reminded Jenny of a fire station. According to her dad, though, it used to hold trains, hence the name.

As they approached, it looked like the entrance and the right door was the exit. Smokers hung around in the middle in limbo.

They welcomed the warmth from the building after their lengthy walk in short dresses. But as they set foot inside the foyer, the air turned damp and sticky, which wasn't welcome. An oversized man and a not-so-much-smaller woman stood at a desk, scanning tickets.

Tattoos covered the woman's upper chest and arms. Meanwhile, the man's favourite place for ink seemed to be his balding head. Neither of them appeared happy as she and Ashleigh approached.

Painting on her biggest smile, Jenny greeted them: "Hi, I'm Jenny. This is Ashleigh. Ethan left tickets for us?" Suddenly excited, she added, "He's playing tonight."

"Good for him," the woman shrugged.

The bald tattoo man snorted and looked them up and down. Observing her own outfit, a bottle green bodycon dress, paired with Ashleigh's pale pink dress, she hesitated. Maybe they had the wrong dress code.

Watching the woman scan an A4 piece of paper that contained a list of names, Jenny fidgeted with her bag strap. Most of the names were crossed out.

"They're good," the woman nodded to the bald tattoo man who, in response, opened a heavy internal door.

"Thank you," Jenny beamed but the bouncers were already dealing with the next set of people behind them.

The sticky air from the foyer dissipated in the large space of the hall, replaced by a chill and deafening music that forced them to shout to communicate. Groups of people were littered across an open floor space. It was early enough that the fluorescent ceiling lights were still on, allowing them to observe the room.

The stage filled a wall on their left, and an opposite wall was home to a long bar that stretched to the end of the room. Hopefully, it meant they wouldn't have to queue long when the music started.

"Can you see Ethan?" Ashleigh shouted.

Jenny looked around again and shook her head. Spotting a cluster of tall bar benches to the bottom right of the room, she pointed them out to Ashleigh, who nodded.

"Start there?" she shouted, barely audible over Korn's *Word Up*.

They managed to claim a vacant bench and Ethan came into sight. He stood by the entrance of the stage, talking to a woman.

Instantly, she grabbed their attention. Alarm bells rang in Jenny's ears.

The woman's black hair was scraped back in a tremendously long, glossy ponytail that hung down her back and swayed with her movements. Chatting to Ethan happily.

A makeup artist? Jenny guessed. Her face was flawless.

She wore a fitted outfit, pointy black studded shoes, tight leather pants and a white blouse that cut off at the shoulders. It was the lowest V-neck she had ever seen, almost stretching to her bellybutton. It screamed, look at me!

"Who's that?" Ashleigh asked, still looking in the same direction. "Is that Ethan?"

Jenny's cheeks flushed. Was Ashleigh thinking what she was thinking? The chat looked intimate and the girl looked hungry, not for food.

Jenny didn't answer but continued watching. The girl placed her hand on Ethan's arm and threw her head back in laughter. Ethan was grinning from ear to ear.

Jenny had to look away. "It *is* Ethan. I have no idea who she is, though." she answered honestly. She hoped she wouldn't find out.

***

Talking to a girl he had just met, Ethan had felt happy for only the second time that day. *Becky, was it?* The first was when Jenny replied to his text. They were only emojis but they left him hopeful he hadn't screwed things up completely.

Becky had found him when he was taking his gear backstage. Matthew would usually be helping but he and Kelly had plans scouting wedding venues.

He was only carrying his guitar case and pedal board when she approached him but he had to put both down to shake her hand.

Her face was as bright as she was beautiful. Like a real pro, she widened her grin and introduced herself as the daughter of the A&R Rep Paul Smith. Ethan blinked at her, not quite knowing how to respond.

"Sorry, what's an A&R Rep?"

She grinned, making him feel a little less nervous.

"Artist and repertoire representative." She didn't make the words sound condescending as she said them, either. "My father couldn't be here tonight, unfortunately. He sends his apologies. He's seen videos of you, though, and is very interested in your music."

She paused, watching him take in her every word.

"I'm here to give him some feedback and take some videos of you in action, if that's okay."

Ethan nodded, the corners of his mouth rose little by little, a delayed reaction to him understanding what she truly meant.

Someone in the industry – a representative. He likes my music!

"Interested in me?" he echoed his own thoughts.

As if she knew what he was thinking, Becky touched his arm and threw her head back, letting out a belly laugh.

"I like you already, Ethan. Just go onstage, do what you do and pretend I'm not even here!"

One corner of his mouth rose in to a smirk. How could he forget a conversation like this?

Connecting the last of his leads, he checked his watch. Jenny should have arrived by now.

From the stage, he looked around, scanning the room that had started to fill. He couldn't pick her out of the groups of people standing around the stage. He had half an hour until showtime. So, tapping his back pocket to check for his wallet, he headed for the bar.

"Hi!" A blonde in a pale pink dress approached him as he stood waiting to be served. He looked around to check she was talking to him. He certainly was getting a lot of attention tonight.

Did he like it?

The approaching bartender acknowledged and served her first. He stood and listened to her order a vodka and coke, along with a rosé with a dash of lemonade. That made him think of Jenny.

"What do you fancy?" she asked him before completing the order.

She looked shocked at the confusion expression on his face
A girl offering to buy me a drink?

93

"Oh, sorry. I didn't introduce myself. I'm Ashleigh, Jenny's friend." Her face warmed as she disclosed the information. "We got a table just over there." She pointed to one of the benches. There, Ethan saw Jenny. She looked at him shyly, perched on a stool. She must have seen the encounter. She raised her hand to him and waved with her fingers and his face erupted into a Duchenne smile.

"Ashleigh, great to meet you." He addressed the barman. "I'll have a Coors, cheers. I'll get the drinks."

He pulled his wallet out of his pocket.

"No, they're on me. Thanks for the ticket, by the way. It's the first gig I've ever been to!" she said excitedly.

"No pressure to be brilliant then," he laughed and turned his back to the bar to see Jenny again.

"Jenny said how good you are at handling the guitar. You're a lucky guy." He felt Ashleigh looking at him but continued to watch Jenny, sensing her nervous energy.

The barman set out their drinks and he turned around to grab them. The pint glass was ice cold and had small beads of overflow running down it. He and Ashleigh both went to grab Jenny's drink at the same time. Their hands touched.

"Whoops, sorry," said Asheligh, looking bashful.

"No, my bad," Ethan replied and offered to take the drink again.

They made their way to the table and Ethan hoped that the argument with Jenny was behind them. She didn't look angry with him.

Thank God.

"Hey, you made it! You okay?" After placing down her drink, his arm naturally rested on her shoulder.

She sat on the tall bar stool, the perfect height for him to pull her into his chest for an embrace.

He almost closed his eyes as she nuzzled into his shirt like she usually did. He gave her body a quick squeeze, hoping it would show her how close he needed her to be.

"Aww, aren't you two the cutest?" said Ashleigh, who had hopped on the barstool opposite, then rested her head in her hand, admiring the intimacy.

Ethan felt Jenny laugh at her with him and planted a kiss on her forehead.

"So, you're the famous Ashleigh I've heard a lot about?"

"I am," she stated. She sipped her drink through a straw before her eyes started to wander around the room. Jenny had told him Ashleigh was a bit of an introvert. Shy. She seemed perfectly adaptable to him, but what did he know?

"So, who was the ponytail girl?" Ashleigh directed at him quite abruptly.

"Ponytail girl?" Ethan echoed her question.

Am I missing a farm reference or something?

"The girl you were just talking to, over there. Who was she?"

Ethan didn't know they had seen him talking to Becky, or notice that her hair was in a ponytail. He felt himself tangle in his own thoughts,

Is she curious or interrogating me?

Noting both Ashleigh and Jenny waiting for his response, he hurried: "Ah, that's some girl. Her dad's seen my stuff before and told her to come along or something."

He shrugged his shoulders and tried to ignore how rigid Jenny's body had become when Ashleigh brought up the ponytail girl.

Should I be worried? he thought.

Ashleigh broke the silence between them. "Shame, I really like the look of her."

She let her statement hang in the air as if waiting for one of them to comment on it. Neither of them said anything but Jenny took a glug from her wine glass.

This night was getting weirder by the second.

CHAPTER 22

Ethan had even impressed himself with the set he played. The buzz of an already excited crowd spurred him on and when it was time to get off the stage, he didn't want to. Unplugging the lead from his guitar, his hands shook with adrenaline

Jenny was waiting at the stage entrance grinning from ear to ear with red cheeks. She must have been amongst the crowd, dancing. Her forehead glistened.

Before he could say anything to her, her arms wrapped around his neck and lowered his head to hers. She kissed him with a force that took him by surprise. Adrenaline already surging through him, his face beamed. They both stepped aside to let members of the next band pass.

"Good job, man," one of them said.

Ethan nodded, sweat still trickling down his forehead.

"You warmed them right up for us!" another boy said as he passed them.

"You were brilliant," Jenny said softly. "You should be really proud of yourself."

Ethan pulled her close again.

"It's all thanks to you," he whispered in her ear.

As she hugged him back, he thought about his grandad teaching him for so many years. Ethan was sure he would be proud. Thoughts of possibilities and where his ambitions might take him clouded his vision.

He had to look for Becky. He couldn't stop here.

***

Jenny observed the crowd around her as they sung along to Ethan's voice and moved to the melodies and beats he created with his loop pedal.

Though she eventually danced along with Ashleigh, she was unable to shake an unwelcome feeling that had nestled in her gut. Hard to define, it was like pride and trepidation were partying together inside her stomach, encompassing her entirety. Pausing as Ashleigh rocked out, Jenny decided to go watch him from the sidelines and take a breather. As she reached the outskirts of the crowd, Ethan began to play the last song of his set – 'Stolen,' her favourite. If she got him alone when he came offstage and had a chance to talk to him, maybe she could squish her churning feelings until they were non-existent. Then everything would be alright.

Everything did feel better as he held her tightly but, before she could take in the comfort of his body, he pulled back slightly and moved from her shoulder.

"Hey, what's wrong? Are you looking for someone?"

He didn't move, just continued to scan the room,

"Oh, Becky. The girl who was talking to me earlier… the one with the ponytail," he added, seeing the confusion on her face. He added the ponytail detail as if it was the most normal thing in the world. The sinking feeling made her catch her breath.

Why are you looking for Becky when I'm standing right here? You're hugging me.

The questions she wanted to, but couldn't ask burned through her mind. She wouldn't let him see her internal panic.

Looking in the same direction as him, she saw Becky stood at the bar.

"I'm going to go get another drink. Do you want one?" she asked.

"No, it's okay. I'll get the drinks," he replied absentmindedly. "You can find Ashleigh."

His gaze remained on Becky.

"Oh, okay." Jenny dropped his hand and walked towards Ashleigh who was dancing by the bench they occupied earlier.

"What's with you?" Ashleigh raised her eyebrows at her. Jenny struggled to hide her distress. "He's got some real talent. You have a Mr Incredible there."

Hearing her call him incredible made her think of the gift she'd got him for Christmas. It was only a gimmick gift. She had just been for a riding lesson on Bluey when she spotted it passing a toyshop window; a Mr Incredible action figure.

The Incredibles was the most recent movie they'd watched. She never thought she would ride a horse but he had taught her. He *was* Mr Incredible and it was the last figure in the shop.

Looking over to the bar where Ethan and Becky stood chatting, her stomach twisted.

"Just going to the loo," she said. She couldn't watch.

Ashleigh nodded at her and held up her empty glass. "I'm off to get a refill." She wobbled, making Jenny laugh despite the worry.

If she carries on like this, she thought, *we'll end up carrying her home.*

CHAPTER 23

Jenny took longer to compose herself than expected. Leaving the toilets, she was sure she had regained control over her thoughts and the suffocating emotions she felt. She tried her best to appear cheerful.

Walking towards a bench where they had previously sat, Jenny paused, her eyes widened. Ashleigh and Ethan were sitting at the bench but were surrounded by a flock of women. Some sat at the bench and the others stood around it. To Jenny, they looked like seagulls surrounding an abandoned tray of chips.

The interlude music blasted through the room, sending ripples through an already buzzing atmosphere.

Approaching, Jenny prepared to elbow her way through to Ashleigh and Ethan, being polite as she did so, of course.

There are so many of them. What was going on?

As she got closer, she saw why the group had all eyes on Ashleigh and Ethan. They were doing a round of shots; five each. The bunch of girls cheered as they got midway through.

Maybe they don't get out often.

As she attempted to manoeuvre her way through, exclaiming "sorry" as she cut her arm through a gap between two of the lady gulls, one of them stepped backwards and knocked Jenny's phone from her hand. The women didn't even notice.

Gritting her teeth, she looked at Ashleigh and Ethan who had finished the shots but were too busy laughing to notice her. Containing a growl, she squatted down low, retrieving her phone. Feeling around the feet of the two women, she was relieved to feel the cool of metal casing in her hand. It was to the left of one of the gulls' heels. She hoped to God she didn't decide to move her foot and tread on her phone or – worst still – her hand as she grabbed it.

Her phone safe in hand, Jenny looked around before standing. She didn't want her bum bumping into anyone in the crowded space. Movement under the bench caught her eye. She froze and her eyes narrowed

What the fuck?

Through the gaps between the gulls, she noticed Ashleigh's hand moving slowly up and down Ethan's leg.

Jenny shook her head, watching as Ashleigh's hand moved higher up his thigh. She squeezed her eyes closed to check she wasn't seeing things, but it was clearly Ashleigh's pink dress. Her hand was now moving back and forth over a bulge that had formed in Ethan's crotch.

Not knowing what else she could do, she stood. The gulls who cackled in conversation were surprised as she popped up behind them. Jenny didn't acknowledge them. She looked straight at Ashleigh and Ethan who had spotted her, too.

Ashleigh gave her a toothy grin and Ethan was expressionless. *Was that panic in his eyes*?

Jenny fought the urge to duck back down to check if what she just saw was still going on. Forgetting to be polite, she passed through the women and pushed herself in between the two that sat opposite Ethan and Ashleigh,

"What's going on?" she demanded, more aggressively than intended.

"What do you mean?" Ethan asked, blinking at her. His expression almost mimicked the others sitting around the bench, all wondering who she was and why she was angry.

Ignoring them, she tried to hold her voice steady.

"Under the table. What the fuck is going on between you two?"

The strangers staring made her temperature rise and adrenaline began to pump through her veins.

Ashleigh raised her hand. It was interlocked with Ethan's. "We're becoming good friends, that's all, see?"

Ethan's expression was still unreadable. Seeing their hands intertwined was too much. Jenny's blood was at boiling point. The urge to hurtle the glasses on the table towards Ashleigh, who winked – *winked!* – was so strong she began to shake. Thoughts flurried through her mind. She stared at Ethan, trying to find some sort of anchor, but his blank face enraged her even more.

What the hell happened? Ashleigh was getting drinks, Ethan was talking to Becky.

Tears pooled in her bottom eyelids but they refused to empty. Looking away, she fumbled to put her phone in her bag. Her phone secured, Jenny trembled but pushed her way through the lady gulls who were excited by the extra entertainment. What else could she do? She had to leave.

She couldn't hurt them, argue with them or ever unsee what Ashleigh's hands were doing. Bile rose to her throat. The image of Cam's mother sobbing on the doorstep as his father drove away flashed in her mind.

Tears threatened to flow as she headed for the exit. Her coat was hooked over her bag strap but she didn't put it on. She hoped the physical sensation of the freezing outside air would dull her aching heart and take her mind off her confusion.

Pushing her fingers through her hair, she tried to avoid eye contact with the people who stood around smoking. She couldn't phone Mam and Dad. There would be too many questions. Taking her phone out of her bag, she dialled Cam.

CHAPTER 24

Jack sighed but it got lost in the noisy, crowded venue. He enjoyed listening to music but an atmosphere where drunken strangers acted like best friends was painful if you hadn't had a drink. He predicted he wouldn't stay long. He was still in his suit from work. So, waiting for Becky to finish a conversation with a guy who just played, he adjusted his tie. The guy wasn't bad onstage but he was delaying Jack's escape. Jack sighed again.

Used to girls wanting him for his money, or to look good stood beside them, he had chosen to relinquish relationships for the time being. He had his date with Becky off for a few months now but when she asked him to go to a live music venue, he thought maybe she was different.

She wasn't. He shouldn't have come.

Jack watched the guy say goodbye to Becky before joining a blonde who carried a monster tray of shots towards a bench. He breathed a sigh of relief. He thought their conversation would never end.

As Becky turned her attention to him, Jack took his car keys from his pocket.

"You're going?" Becky pouted.

He wanted to be polite.

"I'm sorry. This isn't my thing."

"Oh. Wanna do something else? I'm all wrapped up with what I need to do here."

He grimaced and had sympathy for Becky. This bit was always painful.

"I'm sorry. I'm just going to head home. Can I give you a lift or do you have a ride home already?"

Becky's expression hardened. Her eyes narrowed.

Here we go

"I have a lift. Thanks for wasting my time."

She turned and headed into the crowd before he could respond. He didn't mean to waste her time and he certainly didn't want to waste his own. It was another experience that validated his decision to stay away from the women he usually attracted.

"Absolutely, not worth it," he muttered to himself as he headed for the exit.

Following the cobblestone pavement back towards the car, he was glad to be away from the fumes of cigarette smoke that clouded the air surrounding the venue. That's when he spotted a lone woman ahead, her head hanging low, standing under one of the two lamp posts that barely lit the street. She held something in her hand. His eyebrows furrowed. Continuing to walk towards her, he wondered if she was okay. His eyes only moved from her when he caught sight of a group of boys walking in their direction on the opposite pavement.

It only took one of them to notice the woman and the street was full of cat calls: "Need some company, love? I'm the one you're looking for."

"How much do you charge 'en?"

The group's laughter filled the air and adrenaline suddenly surged through Jack. He was close to her now. She was about his age, eyes brimming with tears, her eyes trained on the group now crossing the road towards her. She didn't even notice Jack.

Jack lightly touched her elbow before standing in front of her. He didn't want her thinking he was a threat.

"Walk on, boys, if you know what's good for you."

From their voices, Jack thought they were men but now they were in the light, they only looked about eighteen.

A bald, scrappy looking boy stepped forward to address him. "Sorry, man. Didn't know she was with you."

This angered Jack even more.

"Even if she wasn't, you should have some respect. Would you like me doing that to your mother or sister, eh?"

The group surrounding the scrappy one let out a chorus of ooos. Jack's eyes narrowed and he clenched his fists. The idiot was trying to stare him out. Just before he made a move to lunge

103

at Jack, though, the boy's left eye twitched and he stopped. The girl behind Jack jumped but he didn't waver. The boy knew it was a fight he wouldn't win.

"Whatever, man." The scrawny one shook his head and the group walked on.

"Think there'll be more pull inside?" one of the other boys asked and Jack shook his head.

Degenerates.

Turning around to look at the girl, Jack was surprised to see a small smile edging the corner of her mouth. Tears were still threatening to fall but she looked a lot prettier with a joyful twinkle in her eye.

"Hi, I'm Jack. Sorry for touching your arm. Thought it was the quickest way of seeing them off. You okay?" He took a step back, realising he was still standing close to her.

"Sorry, it's been quite the night." She wiped away a lone tear that fell down her pale cheek.

"You're telling me," Jack laughed to himself. Cam would kill him when he found out that he just blew off the assistant of their newest, biggest client.

After hearing him laugh, the girl's mood seemed to lift. "Thanks for your help. I'm Jenny." She said it confidently and held out her hand. He shook it.

The voices of the group of boys were fading but they could still be heard. Both Jack and Jenny looked at the group as one boy pushed another into the road.

Jack shook his head, "Do you have a lift home, Jenny, or are you waiting for someone?" He recognised the dad-like tone he used and regretted it instantly.

"I've got a lift, thanks. He shouldn't be long now." She looked up the road but there were no approaching cars.

Watching her, Jack felt a pang of jealousy.

A boyfriend? he wondered.

Under the soft orange glow from the streetlamp, her hair looked brown and soft. It hung down in neat curls.

"Thanks for what you just did, it was really kind." He melted seeing dimples form on her cheeks.

"No worries." He looked down and put his hands in his pockets before looking up at her again. "How far off is your lift? I can wait with you if you want me to? The city can be sketchy."

He really hoped she would take him up on the offer. He was curious to see what type of man she might be interested in.

"That would be great if you don't mind." She looked up and down the street, the noises and sounds of the city filling the silence for a moment. Then she said, "So, what do you do, Jack?"

She eyed his suit and he looked down at himself, wishing he had changed.

"Marketing and PR. How about you?"

"Nice, that's the field my friend works in. He's doing well. I'm sort of a teacher, but not," she added. "It's difficult to explain."

"Teacher? But not?" He raised an eyebrow.

"Well, I was an intervention practitioner. The principles are the same as teaching – assessments, planning, outcomes – but I'm supervising other intervention practitioners now. So, I'm not really sure how to describe it!"

He chuckled. "It sounds like you're doing well. My mother's a headteacher. Tough job working with children. You couldn't give me enough money." He laughed and watched a familiar car approach them.

"Jack?" Cam said from the driver's seat, his window ajar. "What the hell are you doing here? Jen?"

"Jack?!" Jenny looked at Jack again. "Cam's business partner Jack?"

She was dumbfounded at the turn of events.

Jack looked from Cam to Jenny and back to Cam.

"Gemma?" He looked at Jenny again.

I was sure she said her name was Jenny.

"No, this is Jenny," Cam explained. "She's my best friend."

"Yep, definitely Jenny, not Gemma." Jenny added.

"Ahh…" said Jack, not knowing what to say.

Jenny held out her hand. "Nice to finally meet you, Jack, Cam's business partner." She giggled. It was good to see her laugh. Turning to Cam, she added, "He saved me from having to deal with giant assholes."

"My main man! Thanks, bro," Cam nodded at Jack.

"No problem. My pleasure." Jack looked at Jenny again and genuinely meant it.

"Date with Becky not go so great then?" Cam questioned, the engine still ticking over.

"Becky," Jack heard Jenny murmur to herself.

"No," Jack inhaled his word through gritted teeth. "Like I told you, not my type at all." He looked at Jenny before looking at Cam again. "Gave it a go, though, hey?" Jack put his hands in his pockets and Cam checked his mirror, seeing lights behind approaching.

"Crap. Jump in, Jen. We've gotta go. Catch up tomorrow, Jack?"

Jack nodded and Jenny got in the car. She gave a small wave to Jack as they pulled off.

CHAPTER 25

They didn't speak for the journey. The roads were quiet and, whatever had happened, Cam didn't feel like they could talk about it while he was driving. All he knew was that Ethan must have messed up big time.

Turning off the engine outside the house, Cam silenced the car.

"Gemma's pulling a double shift again. That girl's going to work herself to death," he stated.

Jenny laughed. "Pot calling the kettle black."

"Come on, let's go inside." Cam got out of the car and walked around to the passenger door. He had never seen Jenny this upset. Clenching his jaw he regretted ever letting her stay at Ethan's. He should have told Jenny that Ethan asked Gemma out the same night he ended up taking her home.

An underlying feeling of unease had developed between Cam and Ethan since that night but seeing Jenny hurt amplified Cam's unease to anger.

***

A strange sensation flowed through Jenny as she entered Cam and Gemma's home, not knowing what might have happened between Ethan and Ashleigh after she left. It filled her with a sense of dread she couldn't shake. The dread followed her, greedily eating away at her. It didn't feel right bringing it into the warm happy home Cam and Gemma had made.

Should I be here? Should I have stayed there?

She followed Cam into the cosy living room which was lit by a single lamp. Remembering the coat and bag she was carrying, she returned to the foyer and hooked them over the coat pegs. She didn't want to mess up their space with her things and she couldn't bring herself to check her phone.

"Want some ice cream?" Cam offered as she re-entered the room. "Isn't that what we're supposed to do? Eat ice cream and talk about what's happened?"

Jenny made the effort and tried to crack a smile but she couldn't sustain it for long. Cam was still friends with Ethan, albeit a distant one since her and Ethan got together, but it was an awkward situation.

"I'll have a cup of tea if you don't mind?" Jenny asked. Her mother always said a cup of tea could solve any woe.

Cam gave her a sympathetic look and headed for the kitchen. As he reached the door, the emotion of the night surged from the pit of Jenny's stomach and rose through her. She gasped, painfully trying to contain the sobs and tears that released, flowing freely down her face.

Cam returned to her in an instant and wrapped his arms around her, containing her racking sobs. The warmth of his fluffy hoody gave Jenny comfort. She sniffled and tried to get a hold of herself. Pulling back from Cam, she used her fingers to dab at her eyes in an attempt to wipe away the never-ending tears. Cam's shirt was full of wet blotches and streaks of black already.

"Sorry about your jacket," she mumbled, stifling the sobs again.

Cam looked down and Jenny couldn't help letting out a small laugh at his insincere expression of disbelief.

"Let me get you a tissue," he grinned, reaching for a box that sat upon a small circular table. Accepting it, she watched Cam sit on the edge of the sofa.

"Come on." He patted it.

She plonked herself down next to him. Her feet were tired. She was tired.

"What happened, Jen?" Cam asked softly.

How could she explain? She didn't really know herself.

After recalling as much as she could, she watched Cam's eyebrows furrow, his expression agitated.

"Sounds like a bizarre night," was all he said, as if taking a moment to collect his thoughts.

108

"So, it's the first time you've been on a night out with Ashleigh, and it's the first time she and Ethan have met?"

Jenny nodded, unsure what to make of his dubious tone. He was either insinuating they might have met previously or he was doing his usual Cam habit of trying to simplify things to work them out. She held her breath waiting for him to speak. Eventually, he did.

"So... Ethan, who we have known since we were kids, and has been in a relationship with you for a while, suddenly enjoys one of your work friends feeling him up in front of you? Or he enjoys knowing you might see?" His eyes narrowed. "It doesn't sound right, Jen. This Ashleigh sounds messed up if you ask me. You're her supervisor right? Could be some twisted power trip she tried to pull?"

Jenny stared at the pale blue rug that filled the centre of the room, taking in what he had said. Jenny didn't really know Ashleigh outside of work.

But why did Ethan just sit there? It's not as if he was glued to the chair, forced to enjoy what was going on under that table.

Her stomach curdled and bile rose in her throat as she replayed the images.

"If you're thinking what I think you are, you have every right to be angry." Cam looked directly at her. "Why would he sit there, let her grab his hand and then not come after you? Bloody idiot." He sat back in the seat and ran his hands through his hair. He always did that when he was stressed. "Sorry, Jen. I'm not making you feel any better, am I? Gemma would know what to say."

It didn't make Jenny feel any better, but his perspective did help her realise Ethan didn't chase after her. Her phone hadn't rung. *Does he not care? Did he like it so much she didn't matter anymore?* Closing her eyes, Jenny prayed that wasn't the case.

Cam sat forward as tears filled Jenny's eyes again. He rested his hand on her knee.

"Look Jen. I'm sorry this happened tonight."

Jenny looked into his eyes. He was refraining from saying something.

What is it?

Cam sighed, "It's not an excuse and only a guess, but maybe he froze?"

She watched his lips tighten and tried to understand what he was trying to say.

"I don't want you to get your hopes up but sometimes fight or flight doesn't happen. Sometimes people freeze. Maybe this was one of those times. Maybe Ethan didn't know what to do to get out of your friend feeling him up?"

Jenny moved forward in her seat and leaned sidewards to rest her head on his shoulder. Cam with his rose-tinted view could be right. It didn't make sense what happened,

"What the hell am I going to do?" she said in a whisper, not sure if she was asking Cam or herself.

Cam placed his arm over her shoulder and gave her a reassuring squeeze.

"You're going to get some sleep in our comfy spare room. Gemma can help you figure out the logistics in the morning. This type of advice is not my strong suit."

Jenny gave him a little nudge with her shoulder.

"You're the best!" She paused, then added, "It would be good to get Gemma's advice, though."

Cam chuckled. "Just make sure you think about what you need and what you want before doing anything. That's the golden, vague advice I'm going to offer."

Jenny wasn't looking at him but knew he was grinning. At least, he was until his phone began to ring. He pulled it from the pocket of his jeans. Jenny couldn't help but look at the caller ID. Was it Ethan? No.

Gemma.

Cam looked at Jenny as if questioning if he was okay to take it.

"Answer it, silly." she demanded, dabbing her face with a tissue, not that it helped her appearance at all.

Gemma appeared on the screen. She was outside the hospital.

She must be freezing, Jenny thought, seeing her stood there in short-sleeved scrubs.

"Hey, sorry. I'm late coming on break." Gemma shivered as she began to speak. "Jen, is that you?" She peered closer to the screen and Jenny leaned into Cam's phone.

"Hi, Gem. Sorry, I've taken you up on your offer of crashing the night."

Seeing herself on the screen made Jenny wince.

I look dreadful.

"Jen – lovely. I'm glad you did. What's wrong?"

Taking in Gemma's concerned expression caused tears to spring from Jenny's eyes again.

Worst night ever.

CHAPTER 26

The next morning, Cam woke feeling like he had a hangover. Seeing Jenny so heartbroken was hard. He sat up and moved to the edge of the bed, thinking back to the last time he cried.

It was a long time ago. He had broken his arm. He couldn't play his PlayStation or go out to play with the kids in the street. He was sitting in his bedroom, alone, in pain, silently sobbing to himself. Having fun was what Cam did. What was he supposed to do when he couldn't have fun?

At the time, there was a little rap on the door and Jenny had come in carrying a mini travel game of *Guess Who* and her favourite stuffed animal, Snuggles the sheep dog. He remembered her face soften seeing him sniff back his tears when she entered.

"Me and Snuggles got bored outside. Will you play *Guess Who* with me?" Cam hadn't said anything as she walked across to his bed and sat crossed-legged opposite him. Nor as she held out the soft toy. "Snuggles is feeling really sad. Can you give him a cuddle while I set this up please?"

With his good arm, Cam had reached for the fluffy dog and gave him a squeeze. He'd smelled like Jenny's house. Jenny had finished setting up the game and watched him place Snuggles in his lap when it was ready.

"Seen as I'm injured, can I take the first turn?" Cam had asked, picking up the first card.

They played until they ran out of people to guess.

"I hope you don't mind but Snuggles would like to sleep here tonight. He wants to make sure you don't hurt your other arm," Jenny had said when they eventually realised she had to go home for tea.

"Won't Snuggles miss you, though?" Cam had asked.

At that, Jenny had looked at the fluffy toy stuffed under his arm. "He's a big brave boy now. He can look after you tonight."

"I'm okay," Cam had huffed. He'd thrown away all his stuffed toys, being the man of the house. But Jenny had left Snuggles with him anyway.

That little sheepdog had stayed under his arm the whole night. Nothing else bad happened to his arm and he hadn't felt sad anymore.

Still contemplating the memory now, Cam walked over to his wardrobe and rummaged through the bottom until he found an old shoebox.

"Hi, Snuggles." He stroked the scruffy little sheepdog smiling. "I think it's time you went home."

As he went downstairs, Cam heard voices in the kitchen. Jenny was already awake and talking with Gemma who always had a cup of Horlicks after a night shift. Entering the kitchen, he watched them both nursing mugs in their hands, happily chatting away.

Wrapping his arm around Gem, he planted a kiss on her forehead. She smelled like she usually did after a shift; strawberries with a mix of sterile hospital scent. She looked tired.

"How are you feeling, Jen?" Cam asked, his arm around Gemma.

"Much better after a sleep. Thank you for putting me up for the night, and for the coffee."

"Anytime. We meant it when we said it!" said Gemma. Draining the rest of her mug, she got up from the breakfast bar, the stool scraping against the tiles. "Like I said, don't take any messing. I'm gonna get some kip but drop me a text or pick up the phone if you need us. Me and Cam are always here."

She looked up at Cam and planted a kiss on his lips before leaving the room.

Cam almost felt like pouting. He hated her working patterns. He was asleep when she was awake and now that Jenny was here, he couldn't climb back to bed with her.

113

"I'll sort you a cooked dinner for when you wake up," Cam called after her.

"You're the best." Gemma called back, followed by the sounds of her footsteps climbing the stairs.

"What's the plan then. Jenster?" he asked, pulling out a box of coco pops from the cupboard. "You had breakfast?"

"Jenster?" she laughed.

"Thought I'd try it. You're right; it's weird." He shrugged and she giggled.

"I'm not hungry, thanks, but when you're ready, I'll take you up on a lift home, or to the train station if that's okay?"

"Course," Cam nodded. Placing his bowl of cereal on the counter opposite her, he took a bite.

"You can make a cooked dinner?" Jenny asked surprised.

Cam was still chewing but held one finger up, gesturing for Jenny to wait as he pulled out his phone. He dialled a number, hit the speakerphone button and, a moment later, his mother answered.

"Hey, Mam. Are you making dinner today?"

"Yes, of course, love. You and Gemma want one?" He watched Jenny brighten at the familiarity of hearing his mother's voice.

"Yes please. Gemma's will have to be to-go, though. She worked last night."

"No problem. Just bring my plates back from last time."

"Okay, Mam," Cam replied, rolling his eyes at Jenny, who was smirking when he ended the conversation.

"You'll sort dinner, eh?" Jenny laughed as Cam continued to eat his cereal.

"What else did you expect?" A cheeky grin spread across his face. There was still sadness in her eyes but Cam could tell she was trying to fight it. She wouldn't have to endure heartbreak alone.

"I've got something for you," said Cam. Jenny eyed him suspiciously.

"Snuggles is feeling really sad. Can you hold him while I finish my cereal, please?" He pulled the sheepdog out of his jogging bottoms' pockets, which were fortunately quite deep.

Jenny's face was a mixture of shock and joy.

114

"He wants a sleepover at your house, too. He's fed up with my old shoe box."

Jenny wiped away a tear as she laughed and held the toy close. It smelled just like Cam's house.

***

Gemma closed the door behind herself. It was a surprise to see Jenny in their house when she called Cam last night, and not a particularly good one. Jealousy nuzzled its way into her when she saw them sat so closely together. They were good friends. Jenny was absolutely lovely and so upset despite her brave face. But wow. It unsettled Gemma, experiencing their true bond for the first time.

"She's staying in your house with your boyfriend because she and her lover have had a tiff?" Hmm," was all Justine, her colleague, had to say to plant the seed of doubt in Gemma's mind. It was stupid. She didn't need to be insecure. She trusted Cam. It had just been a long night. More than anything else, she needed some sleep.

***

The journey back to Primrose Drive was strange. The roads were quiet but, as they entered the Valley, its rolling mountains either side of them, ominous clouds darkened the sky.

Cam knew Jenny was wrestling with her thoughts and that, as soon as he dropped her off, she would be stuck alone with them. Her family was solid but he knew her too well. She wouldn't confide in her parents.

Too cringe.

If he were in Ethan's shoes right now, he would be parked outside her house, waiting for her to get home.

As he drove down the hill, there was no car and no Ethan waiting outside.

'Idiot.'

CHAPTER 27

Ethan didn't make it to bed. His father slamming suitcases onto the stone floor next to him abruptly roused him from his drunken stupor.

"Why the hell is Bryce out there working his butt off by himself?!" Norman's voice boomed, igniting hammers in his head. Rising, he didn't need to see the look on his father's face to know he was disgusted to find Ethan drunk and sprawled on the family sofa. Squinting against the bright light, the large clock that hung on the opposite wall told him it was ten o'clock,

"Shit!"

He felt the back of his father's hand clip the side of his head before he could move. It was already thudding but now it pounded.

"Get your lazy, no-good self changed and help your brother," Norman said. "What the hell is going on with you? Get upstairs before your mother sees you like this."

It was too late. Ethan stumbled up off the sofa and saw his mother gazing at him, her mouth open and her face displaying emotions he couldn't comprehend. He knew his dad wanted to protect her. Her father died an alcoholic.

He didn't say anything to either of them. He didn't know what he could say. After stumbling up the stairs, he took a moment to breathe behind his closed bedroom door, knowing he should be rushing to get dressed.

His mind was groggy, full of questions he needed to ask himself and questions he knew he needed to answer. Thinking of Jenny – her expression when she left last night – cut him from the inside.

116

What have I bloody done?

The working clothes he'd worn the previous day were where he left them on the floor. Putting them on clumsily, he tapped the side of his head, willing for it to clear as quick as possible.

Today was the day he would try coffee, he decided. He needed something to cure this and, if coffee was the best cure, he would surprise his father for the second time today and Goddamn drink one.

Minutes went by like hours, it seemed. They had to scrape the pens, check the cows for frostbite and put down the extra bedding.

The temperature outside had dropped below zero but Ethan had sweat seeping from his pores. Warm and flushed, he ignored Bryce's foul mood. Ethan just got on with the task at hand, grateful for the silence. When they had finished the last of the pens and were about to leave the cow shed, Bryce turned on him.

"What the hell are you doing, Eth?" His tone didn't sound like that of a little brother. It felt like their roles had reversed.

"Not you as well," Ethan grumbled. Taking off his heavy-duty gloves, he flung them on the floor.

"I literally passed my driving test yesterday and you had me drive to the city to pick you up. You were smashed, Eth. Absolutely wasted."

So, that's how I got home with my stuff...

Ethan had wondered how that had happened. He shook his head at himself then smiled, proud of Bryce for braving the city roads to get him.

"And who was that bimbo with you? Where's Jenny?" Bryce demanded, his eyes unblinking.

Ethan took in his brother's expression. He hadn't seen such fury in his eyes before that moment.

"What bimbo?"

He knew the answer but didn't want to lose his brother's respect as well as Jenny's.

"Some drunken blonde bird. You didn't cheat on Jen, did you, Eth?" He looked away before Ethan answered as if scared to find out the answer.

"No," Ethan said firmly. "The bimbo was Jenny's work friend. Things got a bit crazy after a few drinks. She tried to come

117

on to me but nothing happened."

Bryce stared at him once more. "So, where's Jenny?"

Ethan let himself fall back against the wall and slowly slid down it, his body exhausted.

"She saw the whole bloody thing and left." Ethan signed and held his temple. "Dad still got that first aid kit up here? Could do with a few paracetamols."

Byrce walked to the back of the shed. When he came back. he threw a silver packet at him along with a water bottle that hit him squarely in the gut. Ethan groaned but knew he deserved it.

"So, have you talked to Jenny? Did she get home safe?"

Ethan heard the concern in his brother's voice and another pang hit him, even harder than the water bottle. She was part of their family now. Bryce cared for her, too.

"I haven't. I couldn't find my phone after Dad woke me."

He held his head in his hands and remembered Jenny leaving, knowing he never got up to go after her. Ashleigh had grabbed his arm.

"Watch your music stuff," she'd told him. "You don't want it to get nicked."

He was pissed off. She had just felt him up, he had made Jenny look stupid by not admitting it, and now Ashleigh was right; he couldn't just abandon his gear to chase Jenny. Though, maybe he should have. By the time he got outside to look for Jenny, he was too late.

I bet she ran to Cam again.

His fist clenched at the memory. He swallowed a bitter taste that filled his mouth before taking the tablets.

"I'm sure Jenny went to Cam's. She'll be fine," he finally said aloud. "Sorry I was a dick and you had to come and get me." He looked around the cowshed and realised how much his brother had got done without him. "Look, I owe you one, maybe two, even three favours. You looked after me last night and I've been shitty and unreliable."

"Got that right," Bryce said without hesitation. Ethan sighed. What made it worse was how understanding Bryce was being. What he was saying: "Look, I'm sure you'll sort me out when I'm old enough to go out and get pissed. Don't worry about it, okay? Just get your thoughts straight, talk to Jen and, for the love of God, grovel. She's quite awesome." Bryce smirked. "You're definitely punching, you know."

At that, Ethan laughed. "I definitely am."

Sat at the kitchen table with his dad, Ethan was surprised the warm liquid went down so easily. The coffee in his hand was strong but it was a taste he could get used to.

Since he had apologised, the silence between him and Norman had turned from sour to companionable. That was, until a loud shriek from the room above them disturbed the quiet. Ethan and his dad raised their eyes to the ceiling. It was a dramatic shriek followed by sounds of fumbling and desperate rummaging.

"What on God's Earth is that girl doin'?" Norman sighed, exhausted with the drama that suddenly filled their home.

"I'll go find out," Ethan offered. He slid off his chair.

Maybe Emma's having a worse day than me, he thought. Though, somehow, he doubted it.

Walking through the passageway he heard her bounding down the stairs.

"Wow!" was the only word Ethan could use. Unable to keep the surprise from his face, he tried his best not to laugh. Her usual bright red hair was peroxide blonde. Not only had the colour changed; the texture resembled the straw he put down as bedding for the cows earlier, too. She looked like the scarecrow they had in the field, but worse. He wasn't an expert but whatever she had done, it had gone wrong.

Emma glared before he spoke. "Dont!"

Hearing the tone she used. he obeyed. It was safer. "Can you drive me to Marleigh's house? Her mother's a hairdresser. She can fix this."

Pulling a hood over her head, she descended the stairs and grabbed the truck key from the sideboard. She headed out the door and towards it.

"Dad, just heading out. Emma has an emergency," Ethan called through to the kitchen.

"Aye, doesn't she always" he heard Norman grumble.

Ethan followed her to the truck. She was already sitting inside, sunk low into the seat. As he walked across the gravel, a wave of tiredness hit him.

119

Isn't coffee meant to wake you up?

Climbing into the truck, Emma handed him the keys. As he switched on the ignition, an unwelcome, familiar sound drew his attention to the dashboard. The petrol light was on, probably because Bryce had to pick him up from Cardiff the previous night.

Just another reminder of how much I suck, Ethan thought.

"Sorry Em. Gotta stop to get some juice on the way."

She let out a pitiful squeak and sank even lower into the passenger's seat.

CHAPTER 28

After dropping Jenny off, Cam decided to stick around to eat dinner, Gemma would be sleeping until at least late afternoon. Kelly and Matthew managed to make it back in time for dinner so it was a bonus he got to see them. Cam had given Matthew a rough time since the proposal but, after a couple of whiskeys last weekend, they had managed to hug it out and make up. Matthew had been stressed over work and, with the added pressure of proposing, he had Cam as an afterthought, and Cam understood. Kind of.

Kelly entered like a breeze that could catch your breath. They had chosen the wedding venue – Weselton Manor in West Wales – and Cam hadn't seen her this excited since her shop's opening day.

"You'll give me away, of course, won't you, Cam?" She was brimming with anticipation and Cam grinned like a Cheshire cat.

"Of course." He watched her as she jumped up and down with excitement before hugging him.

Wait until she finds out it's one of Plunkett's hotels and I can get a hefty discount, he thought to himself as he held his not-so-little sister for the first time in ages.

"Did you go to Ethan's gig after?" Matthew asked as they sat to eat.

Surprised by the question, Cam tried to act casual. He shrugged. "Nah, too tired and Gemma was working."

He continued to eat and cringed when his mother asked, "Oh, why was Jenny with you this morning if you didn't go? You two hugging outside, people will be thinking you're an item."

Cam rolled his eyes and Kelly stared at him. Cam looked up at her. "Oh she just needed a lift back, I was going the same way."

His tone was firm and didn't leave room for questioning but he knew Kelly would need to dig. She was always weird when it came to his relationship with Jenny.

"So, where did Jenny need a lift from? Why wouldn't she be with Ethan?"

Her face had hardened. Cam ignored her question and continued to eat, though, causing a silence.

"I didn't get a text back from Ethan last night when I checked in. Are they both alright?" Matthew asked Cam.

Cam didn't want to lie and he didn't feel comfortable telling them what had happened. It wasn't his place.

"Don't know why you're asking me," he said. "Jenny was okay when I dropped her off." Kelly didn't question him any further but her eyes remained trained on him. "Am I okay to grab those trousers off you Kel? If they're done, that is? Got extra meetings this week."

"Shoot." Her eyes widened. "They're still in the shop. I forgot to bring them home with me." Kelly pushed the sprouts around her plate. She had always hated sprouts. "I can go get them. I've got lots of work to do anyway." she offered.

"Kel." Matthew cautioned. "You said you wouldn't work."

"Mam did say you're designing a wedding dress for another customer. Well done, Sis.

Kelly looked pleased but Matthews' expression told Cam that maybe Kelly could do without encouragement.

"No, I can pick them up and drop the keys back? It's only down the road," Cam replied.

Matthew nodded in thanks.

Kelly must be pulling some hours if Matthew's concerned, Cam though.

"I can come with you if you want, love?" his mother offered, Cam laughed "Do you not trust me to open and close a back door? Thanks but I'll have some pudding and drop down there myself."

"Who said I made pudding?" his mother laughed.

"I don't mind going down to grab them, " Kelly tried again.

Cam shook his head. "I need to top my fuel up anyway, Kel. I can call in the shop on my way to the petrol station.

"Okay," she said with a sigh. She looked exhausted all of a sudden.

As he grasped the petrol pump with one hand, Cam felt in his trouser pocket for the shop key, checking it was still safe.

A harsh sounding engine entering the petrol station caught his attention. He turned his head to follow the vehicle and saw it was a truck from Ethan's farm. Ethan was driving it. He would have expected him to be hungover or hiding in shame. Cam's eyes widened when he saw a blonde in the passenger seat next to him.

Surely, he wouldn't have been stupid enough to take Ashleigh home with him? Cam was sure Jenny said she was a blonde. *Shit.*

Ethan spotted Cam and lowered his gaze, lips tight in the corners as he got out of the truck.

"You get Jenny home safe?" Ethan asked with an attitude Cam did not expect.

Why the hell is he annoyed with me?

"I did. Good job I did, too. She almost ran into trouble." Cam felt his fists clench around the handle of the pump. "Where were you then eh?" He shot a quick glance at the blonde in the passenger seat. He knew bed hair when he saw it. *Absolute dick.*

Thinking back to the way Ethan reacted to Jenny sitting next to him before, Cam smirked. Placing the nozzle back in the holder, he turned to look Ethan in the eye.

"You always knew she loved having a ride off me anyway."

Cam winked and headed to pay for his fuel, leaving Ethan burning holes in the back of his head. Before the door closed, he heard the truck door slam, followed by the screech of tyres. Cam paid with a large, satisfied grin on his face. He knew he didn't hurt Ethan as much as Ethan hurt Jenny, but it was a good start.

CHAPTER 29

Rage flowed through Ethan's muscles, only escaping through his fists, which clenched the steering wheel in a death grip. He took his eyes off the road for a moment and glanced at his white knuckles.

Keep it together, Eth.

The incessant complaints and shouting from Emma battled his thoughts of the confrontation with Cam, leaving no room to think.

"Why the hell didn't you top up the truck? What are you doing? What if we run out of petrol? You're the worst brother ever! Stop being a dick; turn around!"

Just as he was about to hit boiling point and slam on the brakes, the car started to slow by itself. *Crap.*

Realising the tank was empty, Ethan acted quickly. Pressing on his hazard lights, he used the heavy steering wheel and managed to guide the truck to the side of the road.

"Have we just broken down?"

Ethan looked to his sister. Her mouth was open as shock spread across her face. "This is literally the worst day of my life," she repeated and rested her head against her hand.

"Join the club," Ethan muttered.

"This is all your fault," she snarled at him.

"Shut the hell up, Em!" Fed up with her melodrama, he got out of the truck and slammed the door behind him, knowing she wouldn't follow with her hair the way it was.

Dad will be so pissed I cocked up again.

Ethan rolled his eyes as he dialled his dad's mobile. Norman answered with his usual upbeat tone. All Ethan could manage was a mumble.

"Sorry, Dad. I need a tow."

Kicking a tuft of grass, Ethan thought about Jenny and how karma must be paying him back for screwing up last night. Nothing good had happened since.

Accusatory thoughts penetrated his reflections. None *of this would have happened if Jenny didn't bring that stupid Ashleigh girl, or if she didn't run away to Cam. How the hell was it all my fault?*

His temper was getting out of control again, so he started pacing the grass verge. It would be at least half hour before his dad arrived with the tractor.

Nothing could have happened between Jenny and Cam, could it? Not when Cam was with Gemma and they had been "just friends" all these years? Wasn't Cam his friend, too?

He looked back at the truck where Emma sat pouting.

Cam was a smart boy. If he didn't know what buttons to press with people, he found them quickly. Was his riding comment for the benefit of winding him up? Or was Ethan's sickly doubts right? Was Cam the man Jenny wanted all along?

He lowered himself to the curb. As he did so, his stomach churned with conflict and the throbbing headache threatened to return. Hovering his thumb over her number on the screen, he hesitated. His heart sunk. He was too scared to face any of it. His chest tightened as he turned off the screen.

Once the cold air had sunk into his bones, Ethan decided to get back into the truck, which wasn't much warmer. Emma was silent, staring out of the window at nothing in particular, just avoiding looking at him. It had been twenty minutes since he had called his dad, so he dialled him again to check his E.T.A.

"Sorry, boy. You and Em will have to hang tight. The tractor's cranking but not starting. I'm trying to get her going again."

Ethan groaned. If he had a Jerry can in the truck, he would have walked back to the petrol station. He knew they wouldn't let him fill up without the right container. They would have to wait.

125

"Bryce told me how it's your fault the petrol got used up last night. Serves you right, eh?" Fed up with lectures, Ethan stayed silent. Luckily, his dad continued on a different tack: "I'll get Ol' Blue running in a jiff, don't worry." Norman's voice softened before he hung up.

The cold air and guilt made him shiver.

"Pert Country park isn't far from here, Em. Dad's having trouble with Old Blue. Should we go get some hot drinks, stay warm?"

"Are you mad?" She huffed and stroked her hair again, squishing down the frizz.

"Fine," he said. "Should I go get us some drinks? I'll buy you a flask so it stays warm."

He hoped she would come around. Waiting would be unbearable if she didn't.

"Since when do you drink hot drinks anyway?" Emma asked.

"Since this morning," he retorted. "Do I take that as a yes?"

"Fine, I'll have hot chocolate with extra marshmallows." Emma stated. She still refused to look at him but Ethan was confident she would forgive him. "You still suck by the way." she added as Ethan got out of the truck.

A smug look replaced his scowl. Jenny always said a good cup of tea fixed anything. Today he would test her theory.

***

Jenny answered the phone to Cam. When he told her what he had seen, and what he had said to Ethan in response, the knot in her stomach clenched tighter.

Did Ashleigh really go home with Ethan last night?

It was moments like this in which she needed to think. She always did her best thinking when she had a view to look at.

"Sorry, Jen. I was so angry. I knew it would hurt him and, well, that's what he's done to you, isn't it? He deserved it."

Jenny listened but didn't know what to say to him. Making Ethan think there was anything more than friendship between them, however illogical, was wrong. Especially after their recent argument. She knew it would crush Ethan.

126

Cam said it was a blonde girl. He didn't know what Ashleigh looked like, but who else could it be?

Regardless, it was another girl. Should I care how Ethan feels?

"Don't worry, Cam. It's all good. Just don't imply it again. You know what people think about our friendship already. I'm sure our parents are still convinced we will somehow end up together."

Cam laughed.

"Ah, I think my mother's coming to terms with that not happening. She's taken a real liking to Gemma."

"And so she should. She's a keeper!" Jenny said warmly. She couldn't see Cam but she knew he was smiling.

"I know, Jen."

The phone went silent for a moment, both of them in thought.

"Look, I'm going now," Jenny said eventually. "I think I'll go for a walk and clear my head."

"No worries. Say hi to your parents for me."

Jenny hung up the phone and grabbed her old boots from her wardrobe. It was freezing out but she would be damned if she would sulk in her bedroom all day. She needed a view and Pert Country Park was the closest place with walking trails and a view. Heading downstairs, she beckoned Kiki who was laying on her bed in the living room.

"Come on girl, I'll grab your coat."

As soon as the black Labrador saw the lead in Jenny's hand, she bounded towards her. Attaching the lead to Kiki's collar was easy but her thrashing tail made putting the doggy coat on difficult.

Ready to go, she called goodbye to her parents and headed to the car. Kiki following dutifully behind her.

CHAPTER 30

Excitement filled the air of Pert Country Park. It was full of walkers, and families, all happy to be out enjoying the last day of their weekend. The excitement eluded Jenny. Getting out of the car, she hoped the trails would be quiet.

Following the concrete path leading into the park, Jenny saw children riding bikes around a mini bicycle track. It made her feel happy hearing their laughter. Kiki raised her head in the direction of the dogs that chased and collected balls their owners were throwing on the field opposite.

"Come on, girl," Jenny encouraged as one dog began to approach them. A forest fire road branched towards the forestry and she was determined to get on it as quickly as possible.

Just past it, a coffeehouse caught her attention. Its warm lights shone through the glass doors, beckoning cold visitors to go inside. She would definitely need a coffee later.

The noises of the crowd dissipated the further they got up the fire road trail, replaced by the sounds of birds chittering, trees creaking and wind rustling bushes. She took in the earthy fragrances and started to breathe deeper. It felt good to be outside.

Kiki followed her up the overgrown paths until they came to an opening she remembered. On their summer walks as a family, they would always sit on the bench to eat their sandwiches and watch the world go by in the valley below. Large rocks either side of a familiar bench were damp and covered in moss but the bench was dry for Jenny to sit and enjoy the panoramic view.

Kiki jumped onto the bench and lay her warm head on Jenny's lap. The higher they had got, the colder it was. The resentment Jenny had felt since last night had evolved into a grudge that was settling deep within her.

Will I speak to Ethan again? she asked herself.

Did she need closure on what happened? What did it mean for their future? Did they still have one?

Kiki gave a shiver as the sound of bicycle wheels whirred down the path behind them. Turning her head, Jenny saw a flash of blue before the bike went off path and disappeared between the trees, taking the red trail, a rocky, steep ride to the bottom. Her and Cam tried to walk down it once. It was treacherous.

"Sorry, girl." Jenny stroked Kiki's head before rising. "Let's go warm up." As much as Jenny wanted to, it was far too cold to stay.

They followed the same winding path back down the mountain, the thought of coffee and a cake propelling her. Her anxious thoughts hadn't left her but her head was a little less muggy.

Baby steps.

CHAPTER 31

Every Sunday, Jack and his dad would go on a bike ride after eating their roast. This Sunday, they were in Jack's favourite place: Pert Country Park.

There was a manmade trail that took them from the city to the valley where it was nestled. Today they drove there to conserve their energy for the thrilling trails. His dad had 30 years on him but he still kept up, using his electric bike, of course.

Jack could feel the freezing air against his warm skin. It felt good being away from the concrete jungle. Here he could be himself, away from it all. The meetings, the parties, the expectations.

Navigating the dips' rocky ground helped him feel free. There was no one to answer to, no one to entertain. He could do what he wanted.

Stopping for a drink at the head of the snake-like trail that climbed the mountain, Jack watched clouds of moisture surround his father's face. He held a wide grin through his heavy breathing. They had taken the easiest route up but it was not by any means easy on the lungs.

"I'm going to go on ahead, Dad." Jack mounted his bike.

"Yeah, I'll catch you up," Marcus nodded.

This was a charade they played. Both knew full well that Jack would rush to do the red trail instead of the yellow which was more Marcus's speed.

"Of course you'll catch me up; it's all downhill!" Jack smirked and set off.

Marcus watched him shoot off down the steep hill of the forestry. Jack knew he would be smiling. If Jack beat him to the bottom, they'd agreed, he had to buy the coffee and dessert.

With Marcus not behind him, Jack was free to let loose on the breaks and fly. The wind stung his eyes but it was exhilarating. Following the fire road, he whizzed past someone sitting on a bench. His speed slightly scared him. He spotted a familiar opening in the trees. A wooden post with a red arrow indicated the entrance to the red trail.

Here we go.

The path was tight and he could feel the wheels of the bike sliding on the frozen ground. Nettles nicked at his legs but he lifted the front end of the bike over sharp rocks that protruded from the ground.

His adrenaline surged and, though a gap in the trees afforded him a view, he had no time to look up. The bike skidded and tore up dirt as he rounded a mound of tree roots. The sounds of families in the distance became apparent. He was almost at the bottom.

Leaning the bike against a rack, Jack took off his helmet and shook his head, clearing moisture that gathered underneath it. After clipping the helmet to the bike, he stood up straight and took a deep inhale of cold air, stretching.

There were lots more people using the cafe. They always did at the coldest time of the year. It seemed to peak in summer for ice cream and, in freezing temperatures, people warmed themselves with coffee. Everyone visiting were after the same creature comforts.

The smell of coffee roasting was all-encompassing when Jack entered. Queuing amongst visitors, he felt out of place. They were wrapped up in scarves, women wore full faces of makeup and men were dressed in jeans and Timberlands. In the summer, almost everyone was in padded Lycra with knee and elbow pads, but he was the only cyclist in the café. "Sore thumb" came to mind.

He gazed through the glass doors but there was no sign of his dad yet. He should have been riding down the path towards the cafe, but there was no sign of him yet. Jack was well aware his father liked his leisurely ride back down, taking in nature. He somehow always magically timed it so he arrived when cake appeared on the table. Looking around for a table, he saw that each was occupied. They would have to take it to go.

With four people still left in front of him, he had nothing to do but stare out the window at the walkers and families strolling up and down the park, all of them with different plans in mind. One figure caught his eye. She looked familiar. The image of the woman standing under the streetlight popped into his mind.

Was that her with a dog? Jenny, was it?

She was heading straight for the café. As the queue reduced to three people, Jenny entered. It was definitely her. She walked past to join the end of the line but he couldn't stop himself from calling her.

"Jenny?"

She looked confused at first but, when she recognised him, a smile grew across her face.

"Oh, hi, Jack. Sorry, I hardly recognised you without the suit."

"Not many people do," he laughed. He watched her tuck her hands into her pockets and shiver. "I'm almost at the front of the queue. What can I get you?"

She glanced at the people waiting their turn and looked back to him sheepishly.

"I'm okay. I'll join the back of the line. Thank you, though." She nodded politely before moving to join the line.

"I'll have to guess what you want then," he replied. "Tea, coffee, cake?" It wasn't often he got his offers turned down. This refusal he wouldn't accept.

Jenny strolled back towards him and shrugged her shoulders, the black lab still trained to her side.

"If you insist and it's not too much trouble, a coffee and a brownie would be nice."

He looked at the fly away bits of hair that stuck up around her face.

"Of course, coffee and a brownie coming up."

"I can give you the money, here." She pulled a purse out of her coat pocket but he held up his hand, declining her offer.

"Please don't worry. My treat. I owe Cam enough coffees. Tell him to take it off my tab."

Jenny laughed. At the same time, Jack spotted a couple vacating a small table that had three seats.

"Could you do me a massive favour, though?" He noted how she eyed him suspiciously. "Would you grab that table there for me, please?"

"Of course." Jenny spotted the table and moved towards it, ignoring the eye rolls of the customers queuing behind him.

He was next up to be served but found himself wanting to watch her perch on one of the seats, the dog sat by her side. Noting a bag of dog treats sold at the counter, he picked one up to add to his order.

After paying, Jack carried the three cups of coffee on a tray with an array of dessert boxes and spotted his dad enter the cafe. He saw Marcus eye him suspiciously as he approached the table where a lone girl sat with her dog. Jenny looked up at him as he handed her the cup of coffee.

From the corner of his eye, he saw Marcus still watching him. Jack knew what he was thinking. He had been avoiding all contact with women. If he was involved with anyone, he kept it well away from his parents who were desperate for him to settle down. Jack placed the other coffee and desserts down on the table, aware his father was approaching, trying to eavesdrop. It didn't work, though. An older man in bright green padded Lycra wasn't hard to miss.

"Well, hello," he said. "Who is this, Jack?"

Marcus made a grand entrance, now stood at the end of the table.

"Dad, hey. I got your coffee."

As he spoke, the nerves he felt surfaced so he busied himself, handing his Dad his coffee and cake. He glanced at Jenny who was looking at his dad, smiling.

He relaxed.

It's all good.

"This is Jenny, Dad. She kindly kept this table for us while I got the coffee. She's one of Cam's best friends."

"Oh," his dad pondered. "Cameron? He's a good lad. So, you're Cam's girlfriend?" He looked at Jenny and tried to keep the disappointment from his voice.

133

"No, we're only friends. Cam's girlfriend is called Gemma," Jenny confirmed looking slightly uncomfortable, she began to rise from the table. "Thank you for the coffee, Jack. It was nice to meet you." She paused before adding, "and you... Jack's Dad. Sorry, I didn't catch your name..."

Is she blushing?

"Oh, don't be silly, dear," Marcus added quickly. "There are three seats here and three of us. Sit down. You were technically here first."

He winked and shimmied behind Jack who was still standing. Unable to fault his logic, Jenny nodded and sat back down. Jack watched her take a sip of her coffee. She was quite beautiful.

His father coughed, and Jack realised he was staring. Now sat at the table, Marcus opened the dessert tray and looked disappointed to find a brownie. It was then Jack remembered he was not keen on them.

Oops.

Jack watched the dog lay at Jenny's feet and remembered the biscuits.

"Oh here, these are for you." Jack took the plastic bag from his pocket and handed the treats over to Jenny who looked amused. "Well, not for you. For your dog."

"Thank you. Her name's Kiki. Here, you give them to her." Jenny handed the bag back to him. Jack placed a few biscuits in his palm and held them out to the lab who was whipping her tail with excitement.

He stroked the dog's head after she demolished the crumbs in his palm and was astonished when the dog rested her head on his lap.

"Oh, that's it. You've made a new best friend," Jenny giggled.

Jack saw Marcus smirk before he tucked into his brownie.

"So, how do you know Cam, Jenny?" he asked.

"Oh, we grew up together. He lives – lived – in the house opposite my family." she explained.

"Ah, childhood friends. That's lovely. Him and Jack seem to work well as a pair." He gestured Jack playfully.

Jack laughed, "Yeah I start the deals but Cam's always the one to close them."

"Congratulations on the Plunkett deal, by the way," Jenny said. "I didn't think to congratulate you last night. Cam's excited about it."

"Last night?" his dad asked.

Interrupting the question so neither of them had to answer it, Jack looked at Jenny. "Thanks. It's a big deal."

Jenny nodded. "Thank you for the coffee. Me and Kiki should make a move, though." She rose in her chair and gathered Kiki's lead. "Will likely bump into you again in the future, Jack. It was nice meeting you." Before she could refer to him as Jack's dad again, the older man held out his hand.

"Marcus my dear."

Jenny took his hand. "Marcus, thank you."

"You take care, Jenny."

"See you around, Jenny," Jack added as she went to leave. "Oh, and bye, Kiki."

The dog responded to her name with a tail wag, then departed with her owner.

"She's a nice girl," Marcus said casually when Jenny was out of earshot.

"She is," Jack replied before noticing the brownie box she had left on the table. "I'm just going to give her this. She forgot it." Grabbing the dessert box, Jack followed Jenny who had just got to the door.

***

Speaking with Jack and Marcus was quite refreshing. Their cheery dispositions had rubbed off on Jenny. She held the door open for a lady pushing a stroller and beamed at the little boy, barely visible through a large hood that surrounded his face. Hearing someone call her name behind her, she turned to see it was Jack carrying the dessert box. She had forgotten all about it.

"Your brownie," he said and handed it to her. She took it gratefully with her spare arm.

"Thank you!" she blushed, embarrassed she forgot it. They stood awkwardly for a moment before Jack said goodbye and returned to his dad. Still holding open the door, Jenny looked up to check the coast was clear to exit. She blinked. Ethan was

135

standing there, his body rigid. His eyes sent a cold shiver down her spine. It was a familiar but unrecognisable face.

"That looked cosy," he snorted. "Didn't take you long to move on, eh?"

CHAPTER 32

Power walking up the concrete path with the remnants of her coffee and the cardboard brownie box in her hand, Jenny gritted her teeth. Ethan was hot on her tail. She wanted nothing more than to turn around and scream at him, to tell him to leave her alone. But the families that were entering the country park, all full of excitement and joy, prevented her from doing that. Kiki kept up with her and, from the corner of her eye, Jenny could see the dog shooting her sideward glances as if wondering what was wrong.

As Jenny reached the carpark, she stopped. A car drove past and Jenny saw Kiki look back at Ethan. Jenny knew she was confused but she wasn't stopping to talk. Not here.

"Jen, please…" Ethan called after her as she neared her car.

What's with him trying to be nice straight after upsetting me?

"Just go away," she said. "I'm sure Ashleigh's waiting in your truck, somewhere." She looked around but couldn't see Ethan's truck. *Odd.*

"What?" Ethan demanded. Seeing a couple nearing where they stood, walking into the park, they both remained quiet. Jenny opened the rear car door for Kiki to get in the back.

"There's a good girl," she cooed, stroking her in reassurance before she closed the door.

Turning sharply to face Ethan, she took in his bloodshot eyes and ruffled hair. She had never seen him look so low.

Keeping her resolve, she spoke calmly but assertively. "I don't know why you're here, or why you think you have the right to imply that I'm in a hurry to move on when you were enjoying having my friend feel you up last night!"

137

"That's not what happened!" Ethan interrupted her. When Jenny raised her eyebrows in annoyance, though, he seemed to lower his defences. "Well, yeah… Ashleigh felt me up – but I did not enjoy it! I didn't know what to do for the life of me, Jen. I tried to come after you, almost forgot about my gear. It was stupid, just stupid."

"You're right; it was stupid, but please don't think I am. Cam saw Ashleigh in your truck earlier. Your night didn't end there, obviously."

Ethan's face got red and his voice sounded gruff.

"Cam? You want to talk about Cam? How quick were you to ride off with him? How did your night go? In his house alone? You told me Gemma was working, good timing for things to go belly up, wouldn't you say?"

Jenny trembled. Was he really trying to say she had set up an elaborate scheme? Her voice rose uncontrollably louder.

"I AM NOT ATTRACTED TO CAM AND NEVER WILL BE, IN THAT WAY. I shouldn't have to explain myself to you. I won't let you pin any of this on me."

Ethan cut her off. "Ashleigh wasn't in my truck Jen. It was Emma, and she's still in my truck. She tried to dye her hair blonde. It went wrong. I was giving her a lift to get it fixed."

"Where? The hairdresser's? On a Sunday?" Jenny huffed. "How can I believe a word that comes out of your mouth, Eth?" Spotting an elderly couple with a child passing nearby, she lowered her voice. "Just leave it there, Eth. I'm done." Before he had the chance to speak again, Jenny jumped into the driver's seat of her car and locked the doors. Briefly looking at him to check he wasn't trying to stop her from leaving,. He didn't get in the way. He just stood there, hopelessly watching her pull off.

Coming here was meant to make her feel better. Jack and his dad had made her feel better and then Ethan appeared.

What was he even doing here? Is he following me?

As she pulled onto the main road heading back home, Jenny glanced back at Kiki who had made herself comfortable on the back seat.

"What am I going to do girl!?"

As she continued up the road, she spotted a familiar truck parked on a grass verge. It looked broken down.

Is that Ethan's truck?

Jenny lowered her speed so she could take a good look. That was definitely Ethan's truck and sitting inside was as Ethan confirmed: Emma.

Well, shit.

CHAPTER 33

Repositioning a garment under the sewing machine's needle, Kelly winced. Her head was pounding, almost in time with the machine as she pressed her foot to the pedal.

The engagement party was this weekend.

She and Matthew had been away for one weekend and their friendship group had turned to anarchy. Jenny and Ethan couldn't look at one another, let alone talk amicably, to the point where they hadn't confirmed they had broken up. Assumably, their future together looked bleak.

The catastrophic effect the demise of their relationship had on the group was what annoyed Kelly. Selfishly, she felt impacted the most. She was furious. It had caused a big mess.

Ethan had called Matthew and told him about his encounter with Cam at the petrol station and what he had implied. In defence, Cam told Kelly what Ethan had done to spark his reaction. So, now she and Matthew were disagreeing, both of them taking a side.

Why did Cam let Jenny drag him into her and Ethan's drama? Why did Matthew have to try and protect Ethan so fiercely and argue with her brother?

Kelly was pissed off at both Ethan and Jenny. She didn't want to choose a side. Ethan shouldn't have hurt Jenny and Jenny should have left her brother and the group well out of it.

Why the hell didn't she call me? she wondered. *Isn't that what friends are for? Why rely on Cam?*

Brooke was the only one who managed to stay out of the bedlam. She was too busy being smitten with Dan.

140

Guiding the garment under the needle, she watched the pattern forming. She concentrated on the drumming sound that she usually found therapeutic.

Her and Matthew were solid, but how could they be diplomatic without dissolving their bridal party? After this weekend, having no bridal party seemed like a good idea but Kelly had already started working on the bridesmaids' dresses. She wouldn't let her hard work go to waste over something so silly.

As her anger grew, the thread in the machine snapped. She growled in frustration. Luckily the needle didn't snap.

Abandoning the garment that needed to be finished by tomorrow in case she did any more damage, she rose to make another coffee. Maybe it would make her feel better.

Taking her phone from her pocket as she headed towards the kitchenette, she saw she had a text.

From Matthew x:
Gretna Green?xx

Kelly chuckled. He always knew how to cheer her up, even if he was annoyed with her, too. She slid her phone back into her pocket and vowed to call him after her coffee. He was probably still in a lecture.

Just as she reached the kitchenette, there was a rap on the shop's front door. *Who could that be?*

Walking through to the front, she saw the blonde hair of the bride whose wedding dress she had recently designed. She stood in her doorway with a woman she didn't recognise.

What could she want? Kelly wondered as she opened the door. "Hi! Sorry, I'm closed at the moment. Is everything okay?" Kelly grinned holding the door open just enough to be polite but not enough for them to feel welcome to enter.

She had paid the price drastically for doing that before and had to stay in the shop until 10:00 pm one night. The woman who wanted to come in would not stop talking or leave!

"Oh, sorry. I should have checked your opening times online," the girl said.

Kelly loosened her grip on the door. Clara was being nice enough.

141

"This is my aunt Olivia." Clara gestured to the woman beside her. She had warm, brown hair with subtle blonde highlights and wore a cashmere coat with tan leather boots.

Not that you should judge a book by its cover, but the woman was the type of customer Kelly would try to avoid with a "fully booked" line. Everything about her oozed perfection and, though Kelly loved perfection, she had learned that perfectionists turn into the most difficult customers.

"Olivia Vernon." The woman held her hand out for Kelly to shake.

Very formal. And where have I heard that name?

"How can I help you both?" Kelly asked, fighting the urge to check her watch.

"Umm, well it's a funny story." Clara laughed nervously at Kelly before looking at her aunt.

"May we come in?" Olivia asked. Her eyes seemed to wander over Kelly, making her feel observed. Against her better judgement, she held the door open and let them in.

"I'm just about to make a hot drink. Would either of you like one?" she offered. If this was going to take a while, she should at least have a coffee in hand.

"No, thank you. We won't be here long," Olivia stated, trailing her eyes over the store's gift section. "This is a lovely store. You own it?"

Her wandering eyes had an air of authority.

"Yes. My mother helped me get it started, though." Kelly watched Clara remain near the front door, looking sheepish.

Olivia Vernon. Why do I know that name?

Before Kelly could reiterate her question – "How can I help?" Olivia began to speak: "Clara here, my niece…" She paused. "No wait. It's probably best if I introduce myself properly first, Kelly. I'm Olivia Vernon." She paused again, then added, "Founder and Owner of Caru Ti Bridal."

She watched Kelly's expression change as the penny dropped.

"Oh," she said. *So, that's how I know her!* Caru Ti Bridal was a big deal. Olivia was the designer and driving force behind the brand.

"You can imagine my surprise when my niece here told me she won't require a wedding dress design from me after,

142

apparently, her local seamstress designed one that she simply 'fell in love' with."

Kelly looked at Clara whose cheeks had turned rosy.

It was a real compliment. Olivia Vernon was standing in her shop, annoyed that her niece snubbed her offer, because of what Kelly had already designed. *Eeek! Did she see my design? What does she think of it?*

It was hard to think straight. Olivia Vernon had stores all over Wales and the biggest bridal stores in London stocked her line.

"Ahh," Kelly managed aloud. What could she possibly say? For the first time in a long time, she was speechless. As an afterthought, she turned to Clara: "So, are you happy with the dress design?"

Clara nodded but her eyes gestured to her aunt who began to speak again.

"She was, and I was impressed, too. Not many designs that aren't mine impress me, Kelly," she said unapologetically. Olivia glanced over her workspace behind the glass.

Why am I such a messy worker? Kelly thought.

She winced, seeing the different fabrics tangled on one of the workspaces and the garment she was working on just now, dramatically hanging from the machine.

"I wanted to meet you – find out who this seamstress making wedding dresses was," Olivia continued. "I also wanted to see if she would be interested in applying for a Designer position that is currently vacant in one of my stores."

What?

If they were on the second floor, her jaw might have very well dropped to the first.

"Huh? I'm sorry… You want…?" she stammered.

"I take it you studied garment construction as part of your degree?" Olivia asked, noting a certificate framed and hung on the wall behind the till.

"Uh, yes. It was my favourite module."

"And have you done design work previously?"

Kelly racked her brains: *Have I?*

"I did a little freelance when finishing University but I set up the shop for a steady income. My own wedding got me designing again. I sketch all the time."

143

"Hmm," Olivia nodded.

"The hiring process will be a vigorous one, I won't lie. I only want the best designers working under my name." she said with finality. "The store is located in Conwy. It's a surprisingly vast market up there."

North Wales? That's a little far. Matthew wouldn't be able to move. He was still finishing Uni. Would he even move when he was finished?

Kelly knew his mother relied on him. Despite these qualms, though, she glanced at Clara, who looked as nervous as she felt.

"I don't think I will ask again. Would you consider applying for the position?"

Kelly realised she hadn't answered Olivia. She had to stall somehow. What would Matthew think? What about her own mother? She had investment in the shop, too? Thoughts clogged her brain, worse than the traffic jams on the M4.

"Yes," she announced finally. "How could I say no?" She would be insane to pass up the opportunity to design for an award-winning brand. The learning opportunities were endless. "Thank you. Yes, of course," she repeated with more confidence this time. "Do you ladies want a hot drink now?"

CHAPTER 34

It was the worst Sunday Jenny had ever had. Well, the worst *weekend* she had ever had. Despite Ethan not lying about Ashleigh spending the night with him, she couldn't forget the images and the fact he didn't react to what happened. They still hadn't spoken.

Now Jenny was on her way to speak to Sam, her manager, who had agreed to meet her before the rest of the team arrived at the office on Tuesday. It was fortunate that she and Ashleigh didn't attend the same school on Mondays. Still, Jenny needed to put as many measures in place as possible to limit her exposure and gain control over the situation.

When she arrived at the office, Sam was already making coffee using a large machine the company had recently installed in the centre of their office.

Very nice.

"Want one?" Sam picked up an empty cardboard cup.

"Yes please."

Sam poured a sachet of sugar into his drink while the machine trickled coffee and milk into her cup. He did this with his back to her. Jenny couldn't see his face but there was an awkward tension.

Has Ashleigh spoken to Sam already? Jenny wondered, trying to swallow the panic.

"So, the success you had at Apple Tree Primary, a great notch under your belt, eh?" he said quite merrily with a brief glance should couldn't read.

Jenny placed her bag on the floor at the foot of her usual desk and folded her scarf so it neatly hung over the back of the chair.

145

"Yeah, it was great. The Head was really pleased."

"Sugar?" Sam looked over his shoulder.

"Yes please, just the one." Jenny stayed standing.

How am I going to tell him a colleague felt up my boyfriend, who may or may not have enjoyed it? Shuddering at the thought, she ran through the many ways she could politely request never to work with Ashleigh again. Ever.

Sam walked towards her with the steaming cup "Are you happy to talk if we sit here? There's no one else here yet?"

Jenny nodded and sat down carefully on the swivel chair, holding the hot cup with both hands, distributing the heat evenly.

Sam pulled up a chair with his free hand and sat down opposite her. He crossed one leg over the other and leaned back, watching as Jenny blew on her coffee, avoiding eye contact.

"I know what this is about." Sam declared.

Jenny looked from side to side, *How could he possibly know? Oh my God maybe he had spoken to Ashleigh!*

Sam smirked, "It's okay, Jen. You don't have to worry. It doesn't matter that you didn't tell me as soon as you knew. You don't have full line management, yet."

Knew what? Yet?

Jenny met his eyes for the first time. "What?" Her puzzled expression caused Sam to falter.

"I'm assuming, you were going to tell me that Ashleigh was planning on handing in her notice? It can be really awkward when you're friendly with staff you technically supervise."

Jenny slowly nodded, giving herself a chance to catch up with what Sam was saying. *Ashleigh's leaving?*

"Ashleigh called me yesterday so it's nothing you have to worry about. Annoyingly, she couldn't work her notice. That said, we know you've done most of the work at Apple Tree so me and Pearl agreed to release her early."

Jenny stared at him for a moment. "Ashleigh's gone? Quit?" Her stomach bubbled. It was fit to burst. The relief overwhelmed her.

"Yep." Sam took a sip of the steaming hot coffee and Jenny wondered how his mouth didn't burn.

"We didn't want to stand in her way. I guess you can just keep in touch with her outside of work?"

He raised an eyebrow at the snort Jenny tried to stifle.

"Sorry, dry throat." Jenny coughed and took a gulp of coffee that burnt every nerve in her mouth.

"I am glad you asked to meet, though. I've been meaning to tell you anyway; a new placement has become available and we think you're the perfect fit."

"Wow, what about Apple Tree?" Jenny paused. This conversation was moving faster than she could handle.

"We're hoping you'd take it on. Run the three intervention programmes there and we can ask Brie to cover Apple Tree until we get another staff member."

Jenny wanted to breathe a sigh of relief. If Ashleigh wasn't there, she was happy. Placing her coffee down on the desk, she relaxed back into the chair. This day was turning out better than planned.

"Where is the new placement?" she asked Sam.

He grinned before taking another gulp of coffee. *Does the man have no feeling in his mouth?*

"You'll be pleased to know it's right on your doorstep, actually. Well, not literally, but it's close to where you live."

"Rhiwcymmer Primary, ring any bells?" He looked at her as if expecting a happy reaction.

"Yes, that's where I worked before here." It was difficult to look pleased.

"I thought it was." Sam added. "They need you to go there this afternoon to do an induction. Is that okay?"

Jenny responded to his question with one she had herself. "What ages are they looking at running the programmes for?"

"Years one and two, the teachers are excited."

Years one and two.

Mrs Green usually taught year two. The Mrs Green she left her job to escape. The Mrs Green who was horrid to work with, who loved destroying people's confidence.

Sam paused and looked at Jenny curiously. "Everything okay, Jenny?"

Jenny shook her head and gathered her thoughts.

"All good, yeah." She did her best to sound upbeat to convince him.

"Good," said Sam, who rose and tucked the chair back under its desk.

147

Well, shit, thought Jenny. *Get rid of Ashleigh, get back Mrs Green. Fan-bloody-tastic!* Jenny muttered under her breath and turned on the computer screen. *Time to bury myself in work.*

CHAPTER 35

Ethan had endured total silence from Jenny since their argument in Pert Country Park. It was killing him. He thought of her as he rode on Bluey's back up a dirt path that adjoined fields surrounding them.

Ethan noted Bluey's forward-pointing ears and how the horse blew hot breath through his nostrils, a sure sign that he sensed his rider's stress.

"Sorry, boy." He lent forward in the stirrups to pat his neck and reassure him. "It'll work itself out." Though, he wasn't sure if he was lying to the horse or himself.

Wanting Bluey to feel more at ease on their route to the top of the hill, Ethan relaxed his legs so his hips became supple in the saddle. "We won't go much further today, boy. We can turn it around from the top."

The mist had failed to rise. It hung over the grass and enrobed all it could, dampening the usual sounds that rose from the valley. All Ethan could hear was Bluey's hooves and his own thoughts.

Since things ended badly with Jenny, he and Bluey had walked this route each day. It convinced his dad he valued his job on the farm, and gave him space to think. On the days when the air was clear, he stared over to the opposite hillside. It hurt, but it made him feel close to her in a small way.

He exhaled and Bluey's ears flickered.

Making a clicking sound with his mouth, Ethan gathered the right side of the reins and pulled Bluey around to head home.

"What am I going to do, boy?" he thought out loud. "This week's been difficult."

Jenny still refused to speak to him, his dad questioned his commitment to the farm and Paul Smith, the A&R rep, had a record label called Sound Minds that wanted to sign him.

It's a mess.

Any decision he made would have a ripple effect. If he stayed committed to his life on the farm, he might do so without Jenny and he would lose probably his only opportunity at a career in music. If he chose to sign with Sound Minds then it would inevitably mean his share in the farm would go, along with any chance of Jenny staying with him.

Paul Smith was coming to his house later today to speak with him about the contract and he wanted nothing more than to speak to Jenny about it. It was two more days until Matthew and Kelly's engagement party. Two more days until he would see her again. He was going to have to make the call on his own if he didn't speak to her before the end of the day.

But how can I speak to her? She hates me.

Bluey whinnied and flicked his head as if reminding him they were still standing on top of the cold mountain.

"Off we go, boy" Ethan instructed as they began their descent to the livery. He held Bluey back from breaking into a trot. *This horse loves a thrill. Is that what I want, too? A thrill?*

If he pursued his music, he would have to give up his job on the farm. Hand the reins to Bryce. The prospect of not doing the work was gratifying, but knowing he might disappoint his father – the thought crushed him.

He thought how talking to Jenny would help solve his problems again and felt a pain in his chest.

Why did I lose it seeing her with those two men?

His fists clenched around the loose reins, remembering the younger guy staring into Jenny's eyes as she talked with Kiki's head resting on his lap.

Who the hell was he? What right did he have staring at her in that way? I should have been the one sitting opposite her. Not fetching a drink with Emma sitting in the broken down truck on the layby.

He hated Cam and despised Ashleigh.

"Blame other people all you like, Eth. It won't change your actions. You're the problem," was all Emma had said to him when he arrived back at the truck with no hot drinks.

Venting to his little sister about the argument he just had with Jenny wasn't ideal. Of course she would take Jenny's side. He already felt shit and she made him feel worse.

"What did I do wrong?" he pleaded. "Her friend got handsy with me. Jenny was the one who ran off with Cam and it was Cam's fault I didn't get petrol! Ultimately what the hell did I have the power to change?"

Emma had ignored his defence and self-assurance but it replayed over and over again in his mind. He bit his lip. The moisture from the mist caused his skin to sting with cold, distracting him.

Maybe Jenny didn't think it, but the argument hurt him as much as her. He loved her and, regardless of the time that passed between them, his heart would always belong to her.

CHAPTER 36

The classroom display was the same but the children's faces that were placed in the middle of the class sunflower display had changed. Jenny had recognised a few of the children entering the school, including Rosy. They didn't remember her, though.

It was nice seeing Pat, the secretary, again. She was chuffed she could update Jenny on all the school gossip she had missed. On that note, Joanne had left the school not long after Jenny, two of the teachers were on maternity leave, and the headteacher was retiring at the end of the year. Big changes were happening in the school.

It's a shame Mrs Green hasn't left, Jenny thought as she listened.

Entering the battle-axe's classroom, she held her head high in preparation for encountering her ex-colleague. Jenny paused and turned to check the number on the classroom door.

At a small desk in front of the interactive whiteboard, a woman with bright blonde shoulder-length hair sat facing a computer with her back to Jenny.

Pat said Mrs Green was still in this classroom.

Is this the new Teaching Assistant?

Jenny cleared her throat and walked into the classroom. As the woman turned, however, Jenny's eyes widened.

It was Mrs Green.

The blonde hair made her complexion seem brighter and her sharp green eyes were softer.

My God! Is she wearing lipstick?

The teacher who once reminded her of a Victorian children's nurse now resembled Miss Honey from Matilda.

"Hello, Jenny. Long time no see!" Mrs Green spoke but it was upbeat and friendly.

Who's this imposter and what has she done with that monster?

"Hello," was all Jenny could manage in return. The shock and suspicion of this new version of Mrs Green had her bewildered.

Mrs Green stroked her hair and looked bashful as Jenny stared.

"Oh, yes, I have made a few changes," she giggled.

Jenny smiled cautiously. "Your hair looks fantastic." She meant it. *How is this the same person who ran me out of my job?*

"Thank you, Jenny." Mrs Green began. "Before we start discussing work and the reason you're here, I must apologise."

Jenny's eyebrows furrowed but Mrs Green's positive expression did not falter.

"Apologise? I've just arrived."

Jenny didn't need to fake a confused expression. She had spent the day mentally preparing for an icy cold glare and a harsh tongue. None of it prepared her for *this* Mrs Green, let alone an apology.

"When you were here, I wasn't the easiest person to work with, Jenny. After Joanne left, some friends of mine told me some home truths and I got myself together."

She looked sad as she spoke.

"There's no excuse for my behaviour. My marriage was dreadful. I didn't realise it but I'd soured along with it. And when I heard those home truths, I started rebuilding. Now, here I am!" She held out her hands.

Perplexed at her revelation Jenny continued to stare. What else could she do? Could a sour relationship really make a person sour? Ignoring a stray thought that whispered similar doubts about her and Ethan's relationship, she lowered herself onto one of the small tables.

"You look great! Sorry to hear you were going through a difficult time. Water under the bridge." Not sure if she meant it or not, Jenny just hoped it would be the end of that conversation.

"You look great too, Jenny. Very grown up and doing well. I always thought you'd have become a teacher.

153

"A teacher?" Jenny said, surprised. *You made me feel I couldn't even be an assistant.*

"Yes, you have the way about you. You're great with the children and are clearly capable, being here today."

"Hmm," Jenny hummed in response. She found it hard to take the nice woman in front of her at face value, given that the old Mrs Green had made her doubt herself so much she'd put off achieving her one dream of being a teacher.

Jenny busied herself, looking around the room.

She wasn't sure if Mrs Green detected how standoffish she felt. Nevertheless, a true professional, she pressed onto the matter at hand.

"Shall we talk about the children suitable for the intervention programme?" she asked after a polite pause.

"No problem," said Mrs Green. "They'll be here soon."

Jenny met a lot of the children that day, and made her assessments before finishing the final bell. Hearing the sound of the goodbye song being sung made Jenny pause in the corridor. She was glad the song hadn't changed.

"At half past three, we go home for tea," she sang along before leaving via a corridor. As she departed, she mulled over what she'd discovered.

If Mrs Green found a way to turn herself around, she thought, *maybe I can find happiness, too.*

CHAPTER 37

As Jenny rounded Primrose Drive, she spotted Doreen, her elderly neighbour carrying heavy-looking shopping bags from her car to the house on the brow of their hill, Bert nowhere in sight. So, pulling into the space in front of Doreen's car, she got out to help. The pavements were still icy.

"Hello," Jenny beamed. "Can I give you a hand?"

Doreen was clinging to the handrail of her garden path as she headed back towards the car.

"Oh, love, that's very kind. There are two more bags in the boot."

The frost lay thick on the pavement but, in her boots, Jenny sure-footedly took out the bags, closed the boot and followed Doreen up the garden path.

"Sorry Bert won't be able to come and see you, dear. He's not feeling well."

Jenny watched Doreen look up the stairs. Concern washed over her face.

"Oh, sorry to hear that. There are lots of bugs about."

Is it more than a bug? A horrid feeling grew in the pit of Jenny's stomach.

Following Doreen into the familiar kitchen that was still painted green, she placed the bags on the counter and attempted to hide any sign of worry from her face. She turned to face Doreen who had a lone tear rolling down her cheek.

"Doreen?" Jenny walked over to the lady who used to cradle her as a little girl and wrapped her arms around her. It was upsetting how frail she felt with age. Doreen began sobbing into her shoulder.

"I'm sorry, love."

The old woman pulled away and retrieved a clean tissue from her cardigan pocket. For the first time, Jenny realised that wrinkles covered Doreen's face.

"He doesn't have a bug, love. What he has, they say it's not beatable. Bert can beat anything but he's giving up hope. I don't know what to do."

Jenny's eyes brimmed with tears, the emotional turmoil in Doreen reflected in her. Reaching out, she held Doreen's hand.

"Purple Saxifrage," was all Jenny said to make a glimmer of hope appear upon Doreen's face.

"Bert's favourite flower." Doreen sniffed and held the tissue to her nose. More tears fell down her cheek.

"Yes, and the hardiest flower, remember? Bert would always tell me it's so hardy it could grow in the arctic, beating all odds.

Not sure if she should be building hope without knowing the extent of Bert's illness, Jenny kept her doubts to herself. She couldn't help herself. It was painful seeing Doreen upset.

"Bert's as hardy as that flower, Doreen. We're all here for you.

Doreen sniffed and nodded. She squeezed Jenny's hand.

"Should I pop the kettle on?" Jenny asked.

She wished her mother were there. Coddling and knowing what to say was her forte. Alas, she wasn't. So, putting an extra spoonful of sugar in Doreen's tea (her mother said it cured any woe), she joined her at the kitchen table. Doreen's eyes were red from crying.

"Where is that young man of yours?" she asked, trying to discuss something brighter.

Jenny was disappointed she couldn't oblige Doreen with happy news.

"We haven't seen each other for a while. Umm, things went wrong. We haven't spoken since." She could hear the glumness in her own voice.

"Oh, love, if you and the boy love each other, you'll work things out." She seemed to stare into a memory. "Me and Bert used to have some fallings out, let me tell you. He and the sofa were quite acquainted at bedtime in our first few years." She gasped in a breath before she finished what she wanted to say. "I regret each and every time we slept apart now. It was time wasted. Disagreements feel world changing at the time but in the grand scheme of things, they're just the sneakiest thieves of time."

Doreen finished the tea in her cup and rose.

"Don't let disagreements rob you of your time, Jenny. You don't want to be old like me, wondering where the years have gone, praying for more moments."

The house fell silent as Doreen stood and headed for the sink. A clock on the wall kept time moving. Jenny's heart was breaking for Doreen, for Bert, and for the week she had lost with Ethan.

Exiting the house, she found her little red car waiting where she left it at the curb. She gazed over to the opposite hillside. The black silhouette sat against a backdrop of stars. Her cheeks froze along with her fingers but she stood there perfectly still, her eyes tracing down to the cluster of houses on the farm. The lights were faint but they were there. The memories of the home she had known and the months she spent with Ethan filled her with warmth from the inside.

Taking out her phone, she did what she should have done a couple of days ago: called Ethan.

CHAPTER 38

As far as Kelly was concerned, the storm that raged between Ethan and Jenny had seemed to dissipate, thankfully. It left remnants of debris in the form of bad tension but tonight it was her and Matthew's engagement party. Kelly pulled the silky lavender dress over her head and sighed.

Of course she was looking forward to celebrating her and Matthew's upcoming marriage. Trusting Ethan and her brother to exercise constraint, however, left her feeling dubious. They both had a temper when provoked and she didn't want to imagine them fighting at her engagement party.

There was a tap on her bedroom door and a creak accompanied its motion as it opened. Jenny's head popped through the gap. A warm smile encompassed her face as her eyes fell on the dress that Kelly wore.

"It's beautiful," she said.

Kelly nodded at Jenny, whose head remained in the gap. She looked uncertain about entering.

Fighting an internal battle that threatened to rise through her, Kelly thought, *How can someone so nice attract so much trouble?*

"Come in," Kelly huffed, unable to stifle the irritation she felt. She sat at the dresser and began to add pale foundation to her face. As she did, she made sure to avoid eye contact with Jenny in her vanity mirror.

"I know the timing is far from great but can we talk, please?" Jenny asked.

"Sure." Kelly allowed her eyes to dart upwards as Jenny entered the room. Jenny's sweet perfume mingled with Kelly's zingy scent, making Kelly's nose twitch.

"I never wanted my personal relationships to impact anyone else and certainly not our friendships."

Kelly could feel Jenny awkwardly watching her reflection. She looked up, noting her own stony expression before her eyes met Jenny's. Jenny looked genuinely apologetic.

"I've spoken to Ethan and Cam. They will be on their best behaviour. They know tonight is important and how bizzare this whole situation is."

She paused again before continuing, "Hopefully we can forget this mess and everything will be back to normal."

Unable to restrain the anger she felt, Kelly stood up and faced Jenny.

"You really should have left Cam out of your drama, Jen!"

Jenny's eyes fell to the floor and she moved to slump onto Kelly's neatly made bed. Kelly had the high ground and, it seemed, Jenny was willing to let her keep it. The tension vibrated through the room.

Kelly still stood watching her. It appeared Jenny still had something on her mind. Eventually, she said it.

"I have always been close with Cam, Kel, Cam and Gemma offered for me and Ethan to go there any time we were stuck, I had just witnessed Ethan and Ashleigh... Well, whatever that was. Cam was the closest person. I didn't mean for anyone to get any deeper involved than that."

"But that's the thing, isn't it? You never do mean for people to fall all over you. It just happens!" Kelly's temper rose along with the volume of her voice.

"Sweet little Jenny who never does any wrong. Everyone just loves you, even if you do annoying things that affect the people around you. I see it. I always have!" Kelly took a deep breath in Jenny's silence.

"Do you know how frustrating it is to be around Miss Perfect all the time? My own brother preferred your company over mine and now he's kindling a rift that you and Ethan caused. No one's worrying about my engagement or anything. That doesn't bloody matter, does it?

Jenny shook her head, as if in disbelief. It was clear her own anger was rising but she was restraining it too. Perhaps it was unfair of Kelly to blame the whole thing on her – she hadn't asked for any of it to happen – but Kelly was too furious

159

to think about that now.

"I'm sorry Kel. I'm sorry it all happened. I'm far from perfect! Me and Cam are close because of the imperfections and insecurities we share."

Kelly sat back down and turned to face the mirror. She couldn't look at Jenny but she continued to listen.

"Cam loves you, Kel," Jenny said. "We all do. This night is about you and Matthew, nothing else. No drama."

Angrily dabbing her face with a powder brush, Kelly wondered if she should have done her makeup before donning the dress that clung to her slim figure. Exasperated, she looked back at Jenny with tears brimming in her eyes.

"Kel?"

Hearing the sound of her name caused an outburst of sobs to erupt from Kelly. Jenny moved quickly and cradled her body that was now a blubbering wreck.

"Don't cry. You're not allowed to get splashes over that dress!"

Kelly turned into her for comfort, glad Jenny hadn't got ready yet as her tears began to soak through the Kooks t-shirt she wore.

"I'm sorry, Jen," she said. "I'm being unfair and selfish."

Whether she agreed or not, Jenny didn't tell Kelly her thoughts. She simply continued to stroke her hair and hold her tight.

"You've got nothing to worry about, Kel. It's going to be an amazing night. We're all there for you."

The supportive words only caused the wracking sobs to escalate.

"But I *have* got to worry, Jen. I said yes!"

"Said yes?" Jenny asked, confused. "Of course you said yes. You're marrying Matthew? You're not having doubts, are you?"

Kelly looked up, with streaked makeup, and saw concern on Jenny's face. She sniffed and grabbed a tissue out of a pretty floral box that sat on her dresser. "No, not about Matthew, or the wedding. Matthew is the only one who knows."

Kelly paused to blow her nose.

"Knows what..?" Jenny froze. "Wait. Are you…"

Before Jenny could presume, Kelly rose and closed the door that was still slightly ajar. Leaning against the door, she listened to

160

the silence. Satisfied no one else was in the house, she then paused with her back against the bedroom door.

"I've been offered a job as a wedding dress designer. I said yes."

***

Jenny tensed every muscle in her body to contain the giggle that wanted to burst from her.

A job? Why is she so upset about that?

"That's brilliant. Well done, Kel!"

Kelly looked at her as if she had two heads.

"It's in North Wales. I'd have to close the shop, my mother would have to find a job, my marriage will become a long-distance one. Matthew doesn't finish his degree for another two years."

Kelly stated the facts as if they were a matter of absolute disaster. Jenny's smirk moved to one side of her face, realising that maybe she shouldn't be finding this amusing.

"That is a lot of changes." She nodded sympathetically. It was all she could manage.

"Yep, and I said yes to the job, so I now lose the job or lose the life I have. I don't know what to do."

Jenny took the liberty of sitting back down on the bed no longer needing to comfort Kelly. She tapped the space next to her but Kelly returned to her dresser stool and sat there instead.

"What has Matthew said?" Jenny asked, hoping the cold between them was starting to defrost.

"He was chuffed initially. Realising we'd have to be apart took him a few moments but he still thinks it's a good opportunity."

Jenny nodded. *Right move, Math.*

"He had the brilliant idea of relocating with me after his final year but then it dawned on him that an IT technician job might not be so easy to find in rural North Wales. It's a mess! I can't go."

Jenny could see Kelly was torn from her scrunched up expression. Kelly swivelled on her stool to face the mirror. Again, she began to dab foundation under her now puffy eyes.

"I said yes to Olivia already. It would be such a good opportunity, Jen. I could learn loads! But I'm choosing between my career, my family, friends – everything would change."

"Change isn't easy," Jenny agreed.

She thought of the past week. Some changes made you feel hollow inside, or a hanging sensation in your gut. You still functioned, lived life as usual, but in a state of unfamiliarity. It wasn't nice.

"If you haven't signed a contract yet, you don't need to worry," she said in a bid to provide comfort. "Nothing has to be decided tonight. If you took away everyone else's feelings and decided you would take the job then you could make it work. Maybe your mother could hire another seamstress for the shop? Matthew works with computers, right? Couldn't he work remotely? Just because the job is in North Wales doesn't mean you have to live there the rest of your life."

Kelly's reflection changed and she looked happy for a moment.

"You need to think of yourself, Kel." Jenny mirrored her smile, in both senses of the word. "Everyone else can sort themselves out."

"Thank you, Jen. I'm sorry for being a cow."

"Mooooooo!" Jenny used the deepest voice she could and watched Kelly throw her head back, cackling with laughter. Wiping a rogue tear from her eye, Jenny got serious again. "I will forgive you if you promise to design my wedding dress, if I ever get married."

"Of course, I already have some ideas." Kelly wiggled her eyebrows at her.

"Where do you and Ethan stand now?" Kelly asked. Jenny felt the tiniest thread of a bond starting to reform between them but she was unable to answer Kelly's question, she shrugged her shoulders before responding.

"We've spoken and agreed to put the awful night behind us. But where do we stand? I have no idea."

"Oh," was all Kelly said, apparently disappointed.

"I'm still hurt, but I still love him, you know? Tonight it doesn't matter anyway."

Confiding in Kelly caused a warmth to bubble inside her. Something told her Kelly felt it, too.

"You need to do what's right for you, Jen. Everyone else will sort themselves out." Kelly echoed Jenny's earlier statement and smirked.

"Excellent advice," Jenny said sarcastically. "Now are you going to finish getting ready?"

"Are you going to start?" Kelly bounced back, observing her sweatpants and t-shirt.

"Not until I have a drink with the bride-to-be. Does Jan still keep wine in the fridge?"

"Of course!" Kelly nodded and Jenny headed for the Kitchen.

Maybe things will be okay.

CHAPTER 39

The rugby club hall was transformed. The dated mahogany tables were hidden under white tablecloths and the chairs donned white covers and purple sashes.

Cam was impressed. Kelly had turned this tired room into a modern space for all to enjoy. UV lights illuminated the white and lilac of the tables and disco lights paraded around the room ready for action.

A DJ had a small booth to the right of the stage where a lone microphone stood, biding its time in the hall that was quiet for now. Cam knew who would be on that microphone. Being brutish, he wished the DJ was the only entertainment for the night.

Walking outside the hall, he stood opposite Matthew who waited at the top of the stairwell. His phone screen reflected in his glasses as he replied to what looked like a message.

Cam didn't interrupt. Instead, he stood marvelling at how the boy who always wore jogging bottoms and baseball caps had morphed into the person in front of him. Stubble covered his chin and jawline but he was a sensible computer nerd now. Cam was fond of Matthew. Despite their disagreement about Ethan and his treatment of Jenny, he did admire him. He was doing well for himself and, most importantly, he made his sister happy. Matthew looked older, but they all did.

Putting his phone in his pocket, Matthew looked up. "Kelly's running a little late."

Cam chuckled. In true wedding fashion, they stood waiting for guests to arrive, no doubt Kelly had a perfectly timed late arrival plan. Kelly loved control and tonight they were her puppets.

164

Footsteps sounds from the floor below echoed up the stone walls, followed by something heavy being dragged. Matthew and Cam looked at each other both listening and waiting. There was a sound of something heavy hitting the metal handrail and the grunting of a man.

"Ethan and his amp," Matthew said excitedly. He looked over the banister to confirm his guess. He looked at Cam. "Are you two cool now?"

"I'm cool. No issues with me, bud." Cam held up his hands to reinforce his innocence. He hadn't spoken to Jenny since the day he wound Ethan up at the garage. He most definitely hadn't spoken to Ethan. As far as he was aware, they were still not on speaking terms.

"Cracking," Matthew said before he galloped down the tiled staircase. Did Matthew know something he didn't?

Are Jenny and Ethan back on speaking terms?

Cam peered over the banister and saw the amp Ethan was carrying. The boy could lift. He watched Matthew grab a side of the amp to help.

He must be a fan to help carry that thing.

Cam turned from the banister and walked back towards to the hall's entrance,

"No issues here," he murmured to himself.

As he entered the room, the DJ blasted *Billy Jean* by Michael Jackson. Cam rolled his eyes, he needed a drink.

***

Ethan wasn't sure how he would react to seeing Cam again. He could hardly avoid seeing him now at Kelly's engagement party. The room was dark but his muscles tensed when he saw Cam's figure leaning against a bar at the back of the room. Not even a curt nod passed between them.

Ethan moved the heavy amp towards the stage with Matthew's help. When he had placed the amp down, he could see Cam's white shirt illuminated with the lights. He was moving around the room now, checking the shiny decorative centrepieces. Ethan couldn't help but watch him in the corner of his eye. Looking like he was trying to keep himself busy.

165

The DJ's music was loud. Ethan couldn't hear anything other than Ricky Martin's *Livin' La Vida Loca*.

"Pfft," Ethan huffed not appreciating the DJ's song choice. He saw Cam approach Brooke and Dan, who had just arrived.

He didn't know Dan very well but he was Jenny's ex so, naturally, he hated him. The memory of the day that he and Jenny raced to the swings captured his thoughts. The noise and lights disappeared. He felt like he was in the park again, her smiling as she swung slowly next to him.

Why didn't he stay and talk to her for longer? What would have happened if he did? Could they have gotten together sooner? Would they still be together?

"Hi, Eeeetthhh!!" Brooke screeched as Ricky Martin faded into Ed Sheeran.

He smiled and saluted with two fingers. That's when he saw Jenny enter. She was wearing a long silver dress that sparkled brighter than the centrepieces. He had never seen her in a dress like it.

She looked straight up at him. It was as if she knew he couldn't take his eyes off her. It was hard to make out details in the lighting but his stomach scrunched. There was no mistaking how beautiful she was.

Fighting the urge to go straight to her, he bit his lip and finished plugging in the last of his cables. He would ask Mr DJ to turn his noise down for him to do a soundcheck. Then he could talk to her properly. He had to get it right.

He had signed a contract with Sound Minds who needed him to be on tour for the next half of the year. Convincing Jenny to get back together with him, and telling her about the contract he had signed, would be a challenge. He would have to balance the two perfectly, and he was no trapeze. He was determined he could make it work, though. They loved each other. That's all they needed.

With his sound check complete, he laid his guitar flat on the stage.

"Just grabbing a pint. Will finish the sound check in a second," he hollered to the DJ who nodded, biding time until he could play his party classics again.

The room had filled with a few more early guests. It was selfish. He prevented the music booming again but he needed a quick word with Jenny.

Once again, Cam was propping the bar up, casually watching the room. For once, Ethan wished Cam was standing with Jenny so he could at least get a drink before encountering him.

Ethan adjusted the cuffs on his sleeves. It was better than clenching his fists. *Who the hell makes out they got off with their friends girlfriend?* He reminded himself none of that matters tonight.

Cam was the first to break the stare between them. He turned and called the barman to order another drink. Quickly glancing behind him, Ethan saw that Jenny, Brooke, Dan and Matthew all had eyes on them.

Don't they trust us to be amicable?

Ethan approached and placed his elbow on the bar. Cam held a drink out to him.

"On me," he said. "A peace offering. You were a dick. I was a dick. Truce?"

Cam's grip was tight around the glass. Ethan hated whiskey but he accepted it.

"Thanks." The barmaid looked at him, not sure if he still wanted to order. "I'll have a rosé and a pint of Thatchers, please." The barmaid nodded. "Sorry, bud," Ethan explained. "Grateful and all, but I don't drink the hard stuff." Ethan slid the glass back across the bar. It stopped just before it reached Cam's arm "Rather it not go to waste."

"Ahh," Cam nodded curtly. "Haven't drunk with you in a while. Forgot."

"No worries." Ethan handed the barman a £10 note and picked up the two new drinks he had placed in front of him. "See you in a bit."

Cam nodded and took another sip of whiskey. Ethan made his way towards Jenny.

Time to face the real music.

CHAPTER 40

Heat flooded though Jenny as Ethan approached. Her stomach felt like a popcorn machine, all the kernels popping at the same time.

Calling him the other night had initially made her feel better but the anxiety had built ever since. Ethan was being vague, like he was keeping her at arm's length. He had never been like that before. She felt like hanging up on him, but the tiniest tone of emotion she detected in his voice kept her on the line. They'd chatted until her hand became blue from holding the phone in the freezing night air.

"I'm sorry, Jen."

Ethan stepped towards her now, handing her a glass of rosé, her favourite drink. He glanced around as if to check Matthew, Brooke and Dan weren't watching. Surprisingly, they weren't. Brooke was getting excited about the net above the dance floor that held hundreds of balloons. Matthew had wandered away to welcome arrivals.

"Thanks for the apology and the drink. I'm sorry, too. I shouldn't have told Cam, me being upset is what made him wind you up, I just didn't know what to do."

As she spoke, she became frustrated with herself. Why should she feel bad for telling her best friend what had happened? Or sorry that Cam had hurt his feelings? She was being submissive. Again.

"We both said our piece on the phone, Jen." Ethan eyed the DJ. The entertainer looked anxious, clearly eager to turn back on the music. "Ugh, let me go tell him I actually finished the sound check. I was hoping we could talk without blaring music. Can we chat outside afterwards or something?"

"Yeah, umm, sure" she searched his expression for clues. *What else does he want to talk about?*

"Thanks." Ethan stepped forward and lightly brushed her cheek with his lips. "You look amazing," he whispered. Jenny closed her eyes. The warmth of his lips and his breath on her neck as he spoke made her feel like she could float. *How does he make me so crazy?*

She watched him walk towards the DJ booth. Any reservations she had about them continuing in the relationship had melted away. She wanted him. He loved her. How could one silly night get in the way of that?

The dance floor was packed now the bride-to-be had arrived. Jenny stood at the sides watching the bodies move like a wave. The sight of Kelly's lavender dress caught her eye. She was still working the room, alongside Matthew, their faces full excitement.

Now that's a power couple.

Moving her attention to Brooke and Dan, Jenny saw they were laughing together. Brooke's infectious smile spread to Jenny's face. Ethan watched them too, but stood on the opposite side of the room with Matthew's uncle. His uncle appeared to be talking to himself, Ethan only pretending to listen as he stared at her.

Jenny had danced when Ethan played and she blushed when he saw her singing along to her favourite song, "Stolen." Unfortunate timing meant that all they got to share through the night was fleeting glances. It was disappointing but she had never felt a thrill like it. It was like they were circling each other, just waiting for the moment when they could reunite.

Dancing, Jenny scanned the room and saw Ethan talking to Matthew's dad. *Uch.*

Rhianna's "We Found Love" sounded through the speakers, and Kelly and Brooke, who were dancing next to her, squealed. They had danced to this song in many a night club and, with liquid confidence flowing through her bloodstream, Jenny let loose, moving her hips and shaking her hair along to the music.

Glancing over to where Ethan stood, she saw him watching. He looked handsome in his flannel shirt.

169

The song intensified at the chorus and she looked in his direction. Noticing, Ethan excused himself and headed towards her.

It was hard to stop her loose body becoming rigid. As he got closer, every one of her muscles wanted to tense and her heartbeat tripled. Their eyes locked amongst the revolving disco lights and dancing bodies.

Brooke and Kelly must have seen Ethan approaching. They seemed to drift away while singing to one another. By the time she looked at them and back, Ethan was standing in front of her.

We found love in a hopeless place... the song blared.

Standing steady in her heels, she braced herself as his lips covered hers. Giving in to the natural urge to sustain the moment, she closed her eyes and leaned in closer to him.

"Woooooooo!" Matthew shouted loudly at them as he walked past. He tapped Ethan on the shoulder and grabbed Kelly, dipping and kissing her. There was a chorus of "awws" from the guests around them.

Broke from their trance, Jenny and Ethan laughed at each other. His eyes were shining.

Just before the song beat dropped again, Ethan drew back and did his best attempt of 'big fish, little fish, cardboard box' in time with the music.

Jenny burst into a fit of laughter watching him, as did the others. Then, grinning like a Cheshire cat, he stepped towards her and spoke in her ear: "Stay with me tonight? In the guest house?"

"Yes, please." She nodded and their lips found one another for the second time that night.

CHAPTER 41

Ethan had only had one drink. Jenny had more but was sober enough to feel the zinging tension that hummed and buzzed between them.

Sat in the passenger seat of his car, she thought it would be a while before she felt comfortable getting physical with Ethan but her need for him buried all those thoughts. She craved his warmth and the comfort she felt when he held her.

He placed his hand on her bare knee and the fizzing sensation she felt grew. Placing her right arm on his shoulder, she ran her thumb over his hair. It felt rough as if he had just had it cut.

"What did you want to talk about earlier? We never did get to talk."

She wasn't sure if she wanted to know the answer or if she was trying to distract herself. Ethan knew she only ever played with his hair when she was turned on. His grin told her he thought it was the latter.

"We didn't get to do that did we?" he said, not answering her question.

***

Ethan had been hard since kissing Jenny on the dancefloor. He knew he needed to tell her about leaving for half a year, but right now he needed her body and knew she needed him just as much.

If a person saw them, they would appear to be a normal couple returning from a night out. Together, they casually, strolled to the front door. As soon as the front door opened, though, they unleashed the sexual tension.

"I missed you, Jen," Ethan breathed, pushing her against the front door, closing it behind them. She let out a moan as he lifted her to him.

"I missed you, too," she whispered into his ear as his mouth moved down her neckline.

Arching her back, she moved rhythmically against his crotch, closing her eyes she revelled in the pleasure of the friction.

Groaning, Ethan ripped her dress upwards and pressed her harder into the door. He tugged his trousers down with his free hand, desire turning into necessity.

The guest house keys fell to the floor at the same time as his jeans. He would be damned if either of them slept tonight.

Breathless, they lay awkwardly in the narrow passage. There wasn't enough space to lay side by side so he rested on the right side of her body. His adrenaline started to dissipate. Realising he was probably squishing her, Ethan jumped up and held out his hand to help her to her feet.

"At least we made it through the front door," he smirked.

Jenny accepted his hand up and tried to pull down at her dress. It clung to her body. She would have to find her knickers.

As if reading her mind, Ethan scanned the floor. He picked them up and dangled them on one finger.

"You're not having these back yet."

She tutted but her eyes were playful.

"Maybe I don't want them back yet."

He leaned in towards her and they shared another lingering kiss. Before it could lead them back to the floor, Ethan stretched and opened the living room door.

"Let's grab a drink first." He led the way to the kitchen and Jenny watched him open the cupboard, retrieving two pint glasses.

"You avoided my question," she stated.

Ethan's smile shrank from his face as he ran the kitchen tap.

"I didn't. You distracted me." He felt deflated. *This was going to be anticlimactic.*

"Okay, so you remember that girl Becky, from the Cardiff gig?"

"The girl who was on a date with Jack?"

"Who's Jack?" Ethan asked puzzled.

Jenny shook her head. "Doesn't matter, carry on."

"Okay…" Ethan continued. "Well, her dad is an A&R rep. He was interested in scouting me. That's why she was at the gig. Crazy, right?" Jenny's eyes narrowed and, as if noticing, he hurried past the sticking point. "So, he came here earlier on in the week wanting to sign me to the label. Sound Minds."

Jenny gawped. "A label?"

"Yes, a label," Ethan laughed. "I'll get help with production, gigs, promo – everything!"

Jenny was speechless.

"There is a catch, though," Ethan added. At once, butterflies fluttered in Jenny's gut. "They have a tour set up for a band from England. They're touring the whole of Europe and they need support acts. As a condition, I have to be on that tour."

"Tour? Of *Europe*?" Jenny hadn't been this taken aback in a while.

Ethan – her Ethan – touring Europe? As a musician? He was good but was this really happening?

"What about the farm?" It was the only question she trusted herself to ask.

Ethan handed her a welcomed pint of water, the air began to catch in her rapidly drying throat.

"Dad's going to hire a farm hand. He's said, if I go, he's happy for me, but the farm will go to Bryce. I can't have my cake and eat it."

Was that sadness or relief in his eyes?

"So, you'll be getting paid for the tour?"

Ethan nodded, "Yeah, not much to start but I'll get the expenses, etcetera." He paused. "Only thing holding me back from saying yes, Jen, is you."

"Me?"

"Of course you. I'll be gone for a good couple of months. It's what I needed to speak to you about. I know things have been… well… Do you think you could wait for me?"

"Wait for you?"

"You could maybe come to some of the shows if you could get the time off work."

Jenny hopped onto one of the counters. She didn't want to be standing any longer. *Work?* The thought of work had her mind

173

spiralling. Ethan didn't know Ashleigh had quit. Did he even care that she would have had to deal with that if she hadn't. A lot had happened in a short period of time. She had no idea he had an opportunity to be signed by a label. This was madness.

Apparently ignoring the tinderbox of emotion the room had become, Ethan stood in front of her and wrapped his arms around her waist.

"I messed up and I don't want to do it again. I played my music because of you. I love playing and don't want to stop, but I can't lose you either."

Watching his pale green eyes flit back and forth, she felt a lurch in her stomach.

He was good, really good and she couldn't hold him back from an opportunity like this. But could she be alone for all that time? Not knowing where he is... who he's with? Look at what happened in his last gig, with someone she knew!

"I'm really chuffed for you." Jenny kissed him on the lips. It was a painful relief.

"Oh Jen," Ethan sighed as if he knew where this was going. He kissed her lips softly and, as he did, she felt his body press between her thighs. Her longing returned and the playfulness in his eyes told her he knew it. "Are you ready for bed?"

He kissed her neck and moved his hand between her legs. Breath caught in her throat.

"Will we make it up the stairs?"

He laughed and lifted her down from the counter before he moved away, smiling in a way Jenny would never forget. Taking the two glasses of water in his hands he gestured with one.

"Ladies first." His eyes flicked to the doorway.

Jenny jumped from the counter and headed for the stairs, fully aware he watched her every move.

CHAPTER 42

The sound of rain drifted in through the open window. Ethan crawled up the bed towards her.

"What's wrong?" He was still breathless from all the exertion.

Still laying on the pillows, she welcomed the feel of him resting his head on her chest. Tracing his broad shoulders with her fingers, she didn't know what to say.

Ethan propped himself up on one elbow and looked up at her. "Are you okay?"

"Eth, you can't miss this tour." Anticipation fizzed through her. Was she really about to say what she was thinking? "After everything, though, I'm really not sure being together will be right for either of us."

Jenny wanted to wince. It was like she had ripped off a waxing strip but, instead of reacting with a scream, Ethan was silent, watching her with panic in his eyes.

"No, Jen. I love you."

Her heart broke. *Should I say it back? Would it make it harder? Her a*nticipation turning to dread, she felt the emotions mix inside her, curdling like gone-off milk. He moved to lay beside her.

"Come here," he said. His strong arm pulled her towards him and she rested her head on his chest.

Why was he comforting her when she was saying they couldn't work?

The rain outside became heavier. Its sound soothed the silence. She let herself enjoy the warmth of him underneath her, memorising the sound of his heartbeat drumming in her ear. A single tear rolled down her cheek onto his chest. She knew he was hurting as much as she was.

Does he think I'm right? she wondered.

He squeezed her closer into him. As another teardrop left her face and landed on his skin, Ethan moved to lay beside her and lifted her head.

"Nothing has to be over, Jen. This has been one of the best nights of my life." He looked into her eyes and dried the streak from the fallen tear as he cupped her face. "And not just the sex. Which was amazing," Ethan smirked.

"Knowing I haven't lost you; it's everything to me." Lowering his voice to a whisper, he added, "If you're with me, I'll be okay."

Jenny couldn't stop more tears from forming. His eyes were glassy, too.

Looking at him, in the full extent of this moment, her heart could burst. She loved him truly, deeply. So why couldn't she forget Ashleigh's hand on his leg? Or her crying alone in a street in Cardiff waiting to be rescued.

Why can't I let this go?

Her own advice to Kelly earlier on in the night echoed through her mind: *Do what makes you happy. Everyone else will sort themselves out.*

What would make her happy? Would she be happy with Ethan leaving? Could she be happy without him?

Biting her lip, she snuggled into him and closed her eyes. Did she have to choose now?

"Eth, I'm scared. I love you. You know I do."

Ethan donned a serious expression but still held her tight.

"I'm not sure how we could make it work. You need to be happy – go on this tour – but I can't be part of it."

"You're part of it whether you want to be or not." Ethan sat up. "I got this far because of you. None of this would be happening for me if it wasn't for you."

Jenny didn't want to look at him. Her tears were flowing in a gentle stream down her face. He moved to look at her and she tried to turn away. Pulling her face up to him, he tried to wipe her tears away but more quickly replaced them.

"I can't Eth. I can't be with you."

He looked wounded. She knew he understood. That the finality of her tone told him she meant it.

What else can I say? What else can I do? He needs to leave and I don't want him to.

Tears now pooled in his eyes. "Is us not being together really what you want? I need to hear you say it."

Jenny stayed silent.

"Come on. I need to hear you say it?"

"I'm full of insecurities I didn't have before your gig in the train shack. I can't be with you, and you can't miss this opportunity."

"Say you don't want to be with me." He paused but she didn't reply. "You can be with me, Jen. It's more than an option. I'm right here. Do you want to be with me?"

He was almost frantic now. Burying her face into him, she felt him squeeze her as he held her once more.

"I don't want to be with you," Jenny whispered. Racking sobs followed the words. She wanted to hold him, for him to hold her and for neither of them to let go.

***

Ethan stared out the bedroom window, raindrops on the glass streaking against a black sky. The image ingrained itself in his mind. He had lost her. After a last unforgettable night, she didn't want to be with him. She had said it. He had no choice but to accept it.

He felt sick. He could stay – convince her – but what about the tour? He could lose Jenny and a shot at a career in music if she didn't change her mind.

His thoughts were as tangled as Jenny's hair. He buried his face into it, taking in its fruity scent he breathed in one deep breath.

"I'm lucky to have had you in my life, Jenny Griffiths," he whispered. "I will always be yours. Always."

The rain began to ease. Yet, they stayed curled up with one another until sleep arrived.

***

Cam was getting into his car when Ethan's truck rounded into the street. He jumped in the car and watched it roll down the hill

177

towards him using his mirror.

Movement of Gemma leaving his mothers house caught his attention. Gemma turned to embrace his mother. He loved how they got on so well. He was glad she made it to the party last night, even if it was late.

Gemma waved, noticing Jenny and Ethan pulling up outside the house opposite. Cam turned in time to see Ethan raise his hand in a sheepish gesture and Jenny barely smiled.

Has she been crying? Cam wondered.

Gemma got in the car. "That pair look like they've had happier days."

Cam nodded. "Should I go talk to them?"

He grabbed the car door handle but, before he could release the latch, Gemma rested her hand on his knee.

"Leave them to it. They look like they're processing."

Cam nodded and turned on the engine. She was right; best he not get involved.

By the time he had turned the car around to head up the hill, Jenny was inside her house and Ethan's head rested on the steering wheel of his truck.

Guilt filled Cam. It was never fun to get what you wanted if it meant the people you cared about got hurt.

He reached for Gemma's hand and gave it a squeeze, thinking about when his dad left them.

"Let's hope whatever's happened is for the best," he said aloud. "If they're not right together, it's better they know now rather than when they settle and have kids."

Gemma looked shocked before asking, "Settle? Kids?"

CHAPTER 43

Kelly watched her mother hang the glittering baubles delicately on the branches of the Christmas tree. Maria always loved the day they trimmed up.

Rummaging in the box of various ornaments and tinsel, Kelly's hand hit what she was looking for: her and Cam's Christmas teddies. They had adored them since they were children. They used to play "Santa Claus is Coming to Town" when you pressed their tummies but the music box inside had worn out after a decade of use. It didn't matter though. She and Cam still loved the soft toys. Taking a quick picture of them both propped against the box, she sent it to Cam and abandoned her phone to continue her rummage.

The next item she pulled out was a photo frame of her, Cam and their mother with the caption "Our Family Christmas" engraved on it.

"You okay, love?" her mother asked, knowing something was bothering her.

"Yeah, look at this, Cam still has the gap in his teeth." Kelly laughed and her mother grinned.

"You still have your beauty spot, too," she teased.

"No one calls moles beauty spots anymore, Mam," she said, referring to the mole on her right cheekbone.

"Are you putting off calling her?" Her mother grabbed the last bauble from the bag and hung it as she waited for Kelly's response.

"No… It's just a big thing."

"I know. A good thing, though." Her mother sat on the opposite sofa and rummaged through the box, checking for any rouge baubles. "Change is always scary, but it can be amazing. I can hire a seamstress, so we can keep the shop. You can go into design, gain a wealth of experience and everything will be right where you left it."

Kelly sighed. *Everything?*

Her mother reached over the box and placed her hand on Kelly's shoulder. "Including Matthew."

Kelly tried to feel comforted, Matthew would be there but not with her. They would be starting married life hours away from one another.

"Think about the discount you'll get if you don't get round to finishing your own gowns too," her mother winked.

Kelly's phone buzzed. It was Cam

From Cam:
Frosty and Mike!! We still need to open them up to change their batteries. How good would it be to hear them sing?

Kelly text back,

Sent to Cam:
No way are we cutting my frosty open! I'd rather him be silent than operated on!

From Cam:
You can stitch him back up… you're a
pro

"Kel…" Her mother brought her out of her phone and back into their living room. "Give Olivia a call. You will regret not doing it. You need to go."

Kelly checked the time on her phone, pausing at the sight of her and Matthew on the screensaver. It wasn't five o'clock yet.

"Okay, I will, but no listening"

Maria had tears filling her eyes as Kelly got up and left the room.

Closing the bedroom door behind her, Kelly took a deep breath and hit the dial icon. She had to stand for this conversation. After a couple of rings, the phone answered.

"Caru Ti Bridal, Hannah speaking. How can I help?"

Kelly was pleased to hear Olivia was in a meeting and unavailable to speak.

"I'll get her to call you back as soon as possible." The cheerful girl made Kelly think that maybe she would be that happy if she worked there, too.

Sitting on the bed, she saw a text from Matthew.

From Matthew:
Mam's doing pizza tonight, should we go to the cinema after it?

The thought of pizza made Kelly feel ill. Just before she could respond, though, the phone vibrated in her hand. Unknown caller ID. It had to be Olivia.

She answered and Olivia sounded as chirpy as the receptionist. Maybe they were all having a good day today.

"So, do you have an answer for me, Kelly? Are you going to accept the job offer?"

Kelly couldn't pretend to be happy.
"I'm extremely grateful to be offered such a brilliant opportunity…" She paused, looking at her sketches pinned to the corkboard on her wall. "But I'm very sorry. I have to decline your offer. I don't feel it would be fair to leave my fiancé. If you ever have vacancies closer and would consider me, I'd bite your hand off."

Kelly fought back the tears as she said the words.
I'm throwing away the opportunity of a lifetime.

"Are you sure about this?" Olivia's voice hardened.

Kelly hesitated before confirming: "I wish I could. I'm very sorry."

Hearing the disappointment in Olivia's voice only increased the intensity of her own.

"I'm very sorry too, Kelly. I'll keep you in mind. I wish you well," was all Olivia said before hanging up.

Chewing her lip as if it were numb, Kelly dropped her phone to the floor. She had single handedly flushed one of her dreams down the proverbial toilet.

I wish myself well too, she thought, placing her hand over her stomach.

181

"You better be worth it, little person," she whispered to the bump that wasn't there yet. "I can't believe you don't like pizza."

Picking up her phone, Kelly headed back downstairs. She would tell everyone after New Year's Eve.

CHAPTER 44

Getting out of his father's pickup truck, Ethan pulled his small suitcase from the footwell and retrieved his guitar in its padded case from the back seat. Slinging the latter over his shoulder, he raised the handle on his suitcase and looked at his father who seemed apprehensive.

"Thanks for the lift, Dad."

"Anytime, boy." It was clear his father had never imagined any of his children leaving home. No doubt, he would find it strange, not having his entire family at the farm. But Ethan was confident he would get used to it. They both would. "Sure about this?"

"Sure," Ethan nodded, his breath fogging up around him as he stood in limbo. He didn't want to close the door but also couldn't miss the first flight of his life.

"Make sure you phone us. Keep us up to date."

"Course and umm... thanks, Dad. I know it's been hard on the farm and me messing things up with Jenny."

His dad smiled sadly. "Things don't work out sometimes but it's never over till the fat lady sings as they say, eh? You two might just make it one day. What will be, will be."

Emotions flooded Ethan's body with warmth.

"Thanks, Dad. We can hope, eh?" He tried to look cheerful as he adjusted his beanie hat with his free hand so he could see.

"Safe travels, kid."

"Same to you, Dad. Roads are icy." As he said it, snowflakes began to fall right on cue.

"See you next year!" his dad laughed. *One final dad joke.* It didn't hide his disappointment that Ethan wouldn't see the New Year with them but it lightened the moment.

"Bye, Dad." Ethan closed the truck door and watched his dad drive away, exhaust fumes filling the still cold air.

As he approached the airport doors, his suitcase followed behind him. There, a woman waited at the doors. His heart leapt for a brief moment. *Jenny?*

The shape was all wrong. It was probably someone waiting for a lift. As he got closer, the woman's face became familiar.

"Becky?" It was Paul's daughter from A&R.

"Hi, Ethan. Fancy a travel companion?" She was cheerful even as she shivered. How long had she been standing there? She took in the confused look on his face and laughed, her teeth chattering. "Dad's company wanted someone on the tour to make sure it went smoothly. I was fed up with my job so I quit, here I am!"

Ethan smiled. "You know you could have waited in the warm, right?"

"I could have," she admitted, "but the cold's kept my mind busy. I've never flown before." She giggled nervously.

"Neither have I," said Ethan. "Come on. Let's go. I hope they've got something hot to drink inside."

CHAPTER 45

Seeing Ashleigh shocked Jenny into stillness. Anger and agitation filled her. Standing on a packed train, she couldn't help but glance over and check Ashleigh hadn't spotted her, too. She never wanted to lay eyes on Ashleigh again but here she was, practically opposite her.

Thankfully, she was too busy going over her layers of makeup to notice Jenny among the squished commuters. Jenny averted her gaze to an older lady who sat beside Ashleigh. She wore a green coat with black buttons and was giving Ashleigh a disapproving side-eye. Jenny surprised herself and smiled.

Managing to move her arm just enough to check her watch, she slowly shuffled and faced the other direction. With only ten minutes left of the journey, she couldn't risk making eye contact.

The stop before hers was a hot spot for commuters and the train emptied, allowing everyone more room. Jenny tensed as the camouflage of the crowd vanished. Even if Ashleigh could only see the back of her head, an encounter was something she didn't want to handle.

Moving through commuters loitering near the door, Jenny held her hand over a lit, orange button as the train neared her stop.

It took forever to turn green but she prepared herself for the colour change like she was about to answer a question on family fortunes. The moment it happened, she pressed it, welcoming the woosh of the doors and the icy cold air that hit her face. Stepping onto the platform, she moved briskly away from the train towards a car park.

The further away she got from the train, the more she felt able to breathe. Focusing on the satisfying sound of gravel crunching underneath her boots, and the feel of her bobble hat dutifully bobbing up and down on her head, she focused on getting home.

Home…

It had changed as of this weekend.

She could see her reliable little car at the far end of the carpark, its bright red colour standing out against the grey of the train station and its surroundings. Her car was what Cam called a 'banger' but she loved it. Twisting her key in the lock she felt a familiar click and sighed with relief as its lights flashed. She slunk into the driver's seat and started the ignition. Her warm breath left clouds in the cold air so she turned up the heat to defrost the car and warm herself.

As the frost on the screen melted away, she saw the owner of the very nice BMW return to his car. He looked familiar but the screen was still too misted to see properly. Whoever he was, he drove off as quickly as he arrived.

Not at all jealous of his heated windows, Jenny rolled her eyes and began rubbing her hands together to try and generate heat for herself.

Revving the engine to help warm it quicker, she pulled down the visor and checked herself in the mirror. Her dark brown hair was wrapped up in her hat with just a strand stuck to her face. Ethan used to tell her his favourite feature was her eyes. They just looked sad and sleep deprived now.

She flipped up the visor, the temperature in the car was rising, and the city's LED street lights began to turn on one by one. The screen had now defrosted but tiny snowflakes were already landing on the glass.

Just as she pulled out of her space, she noticed a bright green coat at the end of the carpark. As she got closer, her eyes confirmed her suspicions. It was the older lady that was sitting next to Ashleigh on the train. She was standing on the pavement edge waiting with the snow coming down fast around her.

Jenny gave in to the urge to stop to check she was okay. *It's so cold.*

Rolling down the window, she smiled at the lady in her light dusting of snow.

"Sorry to bother you. Just wanted to check if you were okay? The weather's not the greatest."

Jenny grinned, hoping the lady didn't think she was a weirdo. The expression on the lady's face told her that it had the opposite effect.

"You're no bother, love. I'm waiting for my nephew. My sister said he'd be here and should see me but I think your car is the last in the carpark."

Jenny glanced at her mirrors and over her back shoulder. "You're right about that." She rubbed her hands together again. "It's really cold out there. Do you know where you need to go? I could give you a lift if you wanted? Or you could use my phone?"

Noticing the unease in the lady's face at her suggestion, Jenny remembered she lived in the city now. People weren't as trusting as they were up in the Valleys.

"Umm, it *is* cold. I think I must have missed him." The lady paused again and looked at her small suitcase, "This thing is so heavy, I had to take my time off that bloomin' train. I must have missed him."

Dark patches appeared on the woman's coat as snow leached damp into it. Unable to abandon her, Jenny opened the door, got out of the car and passed her the mobile phone.

"Call your sister if you know her number. I insist. You can't stay here in the cold! If you don't know her number, I can drive you. You can use my phone either way."

The lady looked relieved for the first time.

"Only if it's not too much trouble? The lift? She doesn't live far and you look trustworthy. I won't bother calling her. I can never remember her mobile number."

Jenny nodded, feeling the snow melting on her cheeks. Her car wasn't built for snow but she would try to get this lady home without getting stuck.

"No problem at all. Let me get this in the boot." Jenny grabbed the case, and loaded it into the back while the lady made her way around to the passenger seat. It was surprisingly heavy.

"Very cold out there. I didn't think it would actually snow," Jenny said cheerfully as she got back in the car.

"I know," the lady responded, already settled in the passenger seat. "They never get it right, do they? The one time I want them to be wrong, we have snow."

Jenny laughed "My thoughts exactly. So, where to?"

The lady thought for a moment.

"She lives in Blossom Terrace, I believe it's ten minutes away. Take a left… sorry, I didn't catch your name?"

"It's Jenny."

"Well, thank you very much, Jenny. I'm sure you have a husband to get home to. Oh, sorry you may be too young for that. I'm Ester."

"Very nice to meet you, Ester. Where do we go now?" Jenny managed brightly.

After another fifteen minutes of driving, they found Blossom Terrace. It was unfortunately at the top of a steep hill. The car just about made it up, the snow sticking fast. Jenny began to worry about how she would get back down without sliding.

The houses on this single street were large with double-car drives.

"Number twenty is the house," Ester instructed.

Normally it would be hard to see the house numbers in the dark but, in this street, all the numbers were gold brass and lit, clear to all.

As Jenny stopped outside of number twenty, she recognised the posh BMW from the carpark earlier. It could have been a coincidence but she thought to herself, *Those heated windows made him miss his poor aunt. It doesn't pay to have the best of everything, see!*

"Thank you so much for being a Samaritan and helping me," Esters bright blue eyes shone along with her bright green coat. Clambering out of the car, she turned around to face Jenny. "I would offer you to come in – have some tea and crumble to warm you – but in this snow you need to get to your home."

"It's no problem. Let me help with your bag." Jenny unclipped her seatbelt and got out into the cold to unload the boot. Helping Ester on to the driveway, she was thankful it had been gritted.

"You take care now," Ester said sternly before grabbing Jenny for an unexpected hug. Jenny's first impression of her on the train was right. She was an awesome person.

"Thanks, Ester. You enjoy that crumble for me!" Seeing another car approaching her car from behind, Jenny ran back to the car and gave Ester a wave goodbye as she pulled off down the hill.

Behind the old woman, the light from the front door opened and a male figure greeted Ester. Jenny felt bubbles of happiness. Even the ginormous slide of a hill she had to drive down couldn't stop her from feeling good.

CHAPTER 46

It was almost half past six and Jenny still wasn't home. Starting to feel like a parent, Cam picked up his phone and called her again. It went to voicemail for the second time, and he began to worry. He left the kitchen to check for any sign of her through the living room window that had started to frost. The snow was falling thicker and faster, making the street look like a Christmas scene. Bright white flakes fell against the orange street lamps but there was no sign of headlights.

Wishing she would pick up already, Cam ended the third call at the voicemail. It wasn't like Jenny to be late. It was strange having her live with him and Gemma. He definitely felt like the man of the house now. Not wanting to think the worst, he stared out of the window at the empty spot on the driveway. Gemma would be home soon. He had just spoken with her. Gemma had a good set of wheels.

But Jenny's car… it was so old he had to get her a car stereo that had Bluetooth so she could drive and use handsfree.

Breaking him from his trance, his phone burst to life in his hand.

"Where are you?" he answered eagerly. "I've had to eat all the lasagna by myself. My personal trainer won't be happy."

The smell of lasagna drifted into the living room and he wished the lie were true. He was starving.

"Keep your knickers on, I'm just around the corner. Hope the food is still warm!" Jenny paused. "You haven't really eaten it all, have you?" before he had chance to tease her further she added, "Sorry I'm late. I was doing my good deed for the day and this silly hands-free button wouldn't work. I think it's frozen. Literally frozen."

Cam laughed and saw her car entering the cul-de-sac. Little Red was performing in the snow. The car was as reliable as Jenny claimed.

"Maybe I did a good deed keeping you food, or maybe you'll have to get takeaway…" His voice trailed off as she protested. Cam was glad she was staying with him and Gemma. Her and Ethan breaking up had broken Jenny. He and Gemma could fix it. He was certain.

"See you in a sec." He hung up, watching her car pull into the drive.

***

The call disconnected as Jenny pulled in behind Cam's blue VW. Seeing it always reminded her of the night of Ethan's gig when she had met Jack.

Jenny locked the car and admired how cosy the house looked in the snow. She really hoped Cam had kept her some food. Her stomach had growled several times on the way home.

Taking off her boots, she curled her toes into the thick warm carpet. Thankfully, her socks were still dry. Entering the living room, Jenny's stomach rumbled again as the smell of lasagne reached her nose. Taking the route behind a cushy sofa to the kitchen door, she slowly opened it, hoping food would be on the other side.

Pots, pans and chopping boards filled the counters. Cam was crouched in front of the oven, wearing connected oven mitts like he was about to catch a rugby ball.

"About time," he smirked.

"I helped a lady get home. Even navigated a steep hill in the snow." She entered the kitchen triumphantly.

"How did you end up doing that?" Cam looked surprised. "You know people here keep to themselves." Normally, Jenny would have responded to the sarcasm but her eyes were focused on the lasagna.

"I'm guessing you're hungry?" he laughed as she picked up the still-warm oven mitts and threw them at him.

"I skipped lunch today. I visited three new schools. So, yes, I'm hungry!" Grabbing plates, she placed them on the breakfast bar where they usually ate. Then she slotted Gemma's plate into the oven to keep it warm.

"I've set the table tonight. Had lots of time waiting for you to show up. Gemma wont be long, either." Cam stated almost too casually.

"Gosh! The table. How formal. Is there something you need to talk about?" She looked up and took in his big blue eyes. They were more playful than usual.

"I do." Cam pulled a small ring box out of his pocket. "I picked this out today."

Jenny was in so much shock she dropped her fork. "Cam, oh my gosh! You're asking her? Not tonight, surely?" Jenny knew she was talking fast but couldn't slow down. "Show me! Show me! Show me!"

"Okay, okay."

Cam stood and held out the open box so Jenny could see the glittering Tamora ring inside. Jenny fought back the tears, and it looked like Cam was doing the same. Her best friend was getting married!

Scrap that. Her best friends!

The past few weeks had been rough. She had shocked herself moving from the Valleys. Cam and Gemma had been her rock, the perfect couple.

"I need to know everything!" Jenny demanded. But before Cam could speak, they heard the door open. Cam slid the ring back into his pocket and fake coughed before sitting back down opposite Jenny. A moment later, Gemma entered the kitchen still wearing her hat and coat.

"What's going on in here?" she looked nervous seeing them sat opposite each other in silence.

"Your food!" Jenny jumped up. "I put it in the oven for you, to keep it warm. We were just about to eat. I'm starving!"

Gemma nodded and placed her coat over a breakfast bar stool. "Me too, Jen. Thanks for keeping it warm."

"No worries," Jenny grinned. She glanced at Cam who looked like a nervous wreck.

"I picked up ice cream after work!" Jenny said brightly, kicking Cam back into action.

"You didn't bring it in?" Cam looked confused.

"There's no room in the freezer so I left it to freeze in the car." Jenny laughed at Cam's sceptical expression. She tapped to her head signalling how clever she was.

"Didn't you have your heating on, though?" asked Cam.

"Hope it hasn't melted!" Gemma joined in.

Jenny sat back down at the table with Gemma's plate.

"My hands-free button was frozen in place. My heating isn't that great. Might as well utilise the cold."

Gemma chuckled and placed a kiss on Cam's head before sitting down.

"So, what was this about you helping some lady?" Cam asked Jenny.

Jenny explained the course of events, much to her friends' delight.

"Wow, you're a modern Mother Teresa," said Gemma.

"It was the least I could do."

"Anything else happen on your adventure?" Cam shovelled down his lasagna, but Jenny could see his hand rested on his jeans pocket.

"I saw Ashleigh on the train," Jenny blurted.

That should take his mind off the ring.

Saying it aloud made her insides hurt and she realised she had turned the vibrant conversation sombre. "She didn't see me, thankfully. It was going to happen at some point. Just didn't expect it today. Still, it's done now."

Good save, Jen.

"It's definitely been a day then. Are you ok?" Gemma asked.

Don't cry, don't cry, Jenny pleaded with herself. She put on a stoic façade.

"I'm okay. Just, you know… getting on with it." She stopped eating and took her dish over to the sink. Leaving the kitchen before she crumbled, she added, "I'll go get the ice cream for dessert!"

CHAPTER 47

(Four Months Later)

Jack was sitting in the booth he and Cam always sat in when they came to Joey's. The only place in the city that had the right balance of booze and fun.

He thought back to when he forgot he was meant to collect his Aunt Ester from the station after work. He was just about to race out to get her but, when he opened the front door, she was standing in the middle of their driveway, embracing Cam's friend Jenny.

The same Jenny he hadn't been able to get out his thoughts since meeting her.

In the moment of shock, he wanted to call her. To tell her to wait so he could speak to her. But by the time his aunt greeted him, Jenny was driving away in a little red car. He hadn't stopped thinking about her since.

He expected Cam to talk about Jenny more often than he did. He wasn't sure if he knew they had met at Pert Country Park. It was Gemma who seemed keen to introduce them in a dating capacity. He owed her one for setting it all up.

Sitting in the booth, a drink in hand, he wondered if he would bring it up that it was her who had saved his aunt from the snow. *Or should I play it cool?* He was purposefully early to make sure he decided before she arrived.

His dad's voice played over in his mind: *Get a girl, settle down, stop wasting your time. There's more to life than work.*

It grated on him. He hadn't mentioned it was Jenny he saw outside the house to his dad. Since they had bumped into her in Pert Country Park, his dad had fixated on her as much as Jack.

194

Telling his dad they would be going on a blind date would send him into a frenzy. And did he *really* want to be going on a date with her? He knew he couldn't resist seeing her again, even if he wanted to avoid it.

Jack checked his watch and, when he looked up, the door of Joey's opened. He expected to see Cam and Gemma enter first, Cam with an awkward smile and Gemma with her pearly white grin, but it was Jenny.

Wearing a snug v-neck dress, paired with golden ballet pumps and a necklace to match, she took his breath away.

"Hi, Jack," she said. "It's nice to see you again."

The End

FOLLOW KAYLEIGH ONLINE

Dear Reader,

Lots of authors have a mailing list to keep their readers up to date on their latest releases. As I'm new to this author gig, I don't have a list yet but you can follow me on Instagram. Do so and you'll be the first to hear about the list when it materialises. Plus, you'll get some free goodies when I've finished creating them. Find me at:

@kayleigh_evans_author.94

Kind regards,
Kayleigh

ALSO BY
KAYLEIGH EVANS

Serendipity Valley: How It Begins is Kayleigh's debut novel. However, she plans to bring out more soon and might have already done so by the time you read this message. For more information, visit:

KayleighEvansAuthor.com

Printed in Great Britain
by Amazon